Prior Praise for Rick Rofihe's Work

"These surgically precise slices of intelligent life are distinguished by virtuosic phrase-making and fetchingly off-beat specifics."

—Bruce Allen, *The New York Times Book Review*

"Mr. Rofihe can be surprisingly effective, with a quirky tenderness. Oddly touching, the interest here lies not in the stories' mundane incidents, but in things barely hinted at: beneath this calm surface, powerful currents flow."

—Bruce Bawer, *The Wall Street Journal*

"Rick Rofihe's stories have bulging motor nerves and threadlike muscles. They are contour almost without mass; lines of fierce magnetic energy with only a dusting of iron fillings to reveal their course. They are elusive, but not in the sense of escaping us. It is more as if we are unable to find them, and then they spring out at us; we are not sure from where."

—Richard Eder, *The Los Angeles Times*

"A gentle but insistent touch.... Rofihe pays close attention to how people talk about what they think and do."

—*Publishers Weekly*

"Rofihe speaks convincingly in many voices. His characters are absolutely believable, and the kind you wouldn't cross the street to avoid meeting."

—Gregory McNamee, *Washington Post Book World*

"The narratives weave toward minor epiphanies, backing and filling, curving around their characters with a seeming lack of coherence—yet they are strangely compelling, as the refusal to make plain their meanings gives more depth to implication."

—Michael Darling, *Books in Canada*

"What makes him different from some of the other successfully quirky writers? The difference seems to be one of commitment; he takes the big risks so many stylists never do. Without moralizing, Rofihe judges. His nose quivers at a new odor in the emotional air, and he makes a guess at what it is. Like all the good poets, he's there to name things—in his case, things most of us don't even notice."

—Marianne Ackerman, *The Montreal Gazette*

"Each of Rofihe's stories is a puzzle you want to solve, and you smile when you do. Communication in one form or another is the key to these playful warm tales. A fresh, funny, and deeply felt collection."

—Donna Seaman, *American Library Association*

"Life's victories and defeats are measured by little moments and insights. But in the stories of Rick Rofihe they become unusually dense, compact fictions that resist easy reading and quick retelling almost as much as they resist leaving your memory."

—Jacob Stockinger, *The Madison (Wisconsin) Capitol Times*

"The proof of true mastery is making what's difficult look easy. Rofihe has a real knack for telling a convincing story; instead of playing the puppetmaster, he becomes the puppet itself, breathing life into each character. These stories are rich in detail, nuance and feeling, each a separate gem in its own modest way."

—*Library Journal*

"Most of these stories are told in the first person by characters who are unsure of their thoughts' importance, who are searching for explanations. In their narratives, the trivial and comic jostle the momentous. *Uneasiness* hangs over every scene, a chronic strange vibration, but all are enormously sympathetic, and their courage and humour haunt like sad music. (All the stories would be wonderful to hear read aloud.) Every sentence—cryptic as it may be— both rings true and sounds poetic, as if some massive emotional significance is close by, only a paragraph away. No words are wasted. These are small, quiet stories, serious, sophisticated, and evocative. This is a literary book."

—Russell Smith, *Quill & Quire*

"Rick Rofihe's short stories are very sophisticated indeed, and it comes as no surprise to learn that they have appeared in *The New Yorker.* He is a talented writer whose versatility and empathetic sensibility are remarkable. This is serious literature."

—Joan McGrath, *CM*, Canadian Library Association

"Confident in his reach... he dazzles."

—*Kirkus Reviews*

"... brief, mostly first-person stories about the riddles of communication and the grammar of loneliness. Rofihe's oblique narratives are coded messages, waiting to be deciphered."

—*The New Yorker*

Also by Rick Rofihe

FATHER MUST: STORIES
                    – Farrar, Straus and Giroux

BOYS WHO DO THE BOP

Collected Short Stories

RICK ROFIHE

Mercer Street Books

First Printed 2023 Copyright © by Rick Rofihe. All rights reserved. Printed in the United States of America by Mercer Street Books Publishing, New York.
pub@mercerstreetbooks.com
ISBN 978-1-958576-03-8

"Boys Who Do the Bop," "Father Must," "Satellite Dish," "Elevator Neighbors," "Read Chinese," "Cousin," "Yellow Dining Room," "Jelly Doughnuts" and "Carmen" were originally published in *The New Yorker;* "Six Quarters," "Quiet" and "Born Here" in *Grand Street;* "Feeling Marlene" and "Eidetic" in *Open City;* "Chicagoo" in *Swink;* "Three Point Back" in *Epiphany;* "Australia" on *slushpilemag.com;* "Frederick" in *Unsaid;* "Tangenital," "Me. You. Love" and "Scar" on *anderbo.com;* "Things We Say to Cops (Things Cops Say to Us)" and "The Bowery Scene" on *mrbellersneighborhood.com;* "Northeast of Eden" in *The New York Times;* "Saturday Birthdays," "Something about Ireland," "A Lot of Things to Tell You," "Helen Says" and "Snowsuit" in FATHER MUST by Rick Rofihe and published by Farrar, Straus and Giroux.

BOYS WHO
DO THE BOP

CONTENTS

BOYS WHO DO THE BOP

Learning to type? Not easy, right?

```
It is work which gives flavor to life.
It is work which gives flavor to life.
It is work which gives flavor to life.
```

It can't be easy, with the letters presented to you shuffled up the way they are. Few typing instructors will concede that there's any disarray, but at least half the instruction books I've seen feature practice sentences that try to play up the learner's sense of purpose and foster a feeling of order where there's apparently none.

Enid is in her room putting on makeup. Why do anything to those delicate features? "Because it takes up time," she would say if asked.

Enid closes her bedroom door when she changes her clothes but leaves it ajar when she's doing her face; is she hoping some small talk might reach her dainty ears? If that's so, and if I am to oblige, I have to keep one eye on the keyboard, one eye on that door. Have I been much too quiet already? It must be so, for she's starting to sing.

I've been across this country clear
from Bangor, Maine, to Frisco, where
I turned around,
feet on the ground,
and headed back on home somehow

That's a good song; why would I want to interrupt it? Besides, typing requires concentrated practice.

```
Do the thing and you have still the power; but
they who do not the thing have not the power.
```

Soon she says, "Oh you want more floor show?"

When Lady Luck would treat me right,
I'd hit some town on a Saturday night,
and rule of thumb
where I come from
is party time is now. I'm—

She stops making up in her oval dresser mirror and comes out to look in the full-length one.

"These pants are too... what is the word, Noonie? Or cats got tongue?"

I like Enid, and I like just about anything Enid says to me, and I'd just as soon hang around here with her and her cats as just about anything, maybe anything. Now, to talk or to type?

```
If you would not be forgotten, as soon as you
are dead and rotten, either write things worth
reading or
```

"Unable to wear THESE pants at THIS time," she says, and walks back into her room and closes the door.

This is the longest I've stayed at Enid's, six weeks now. The sofa here is certainly comfortable; I prefer it to the bed in the spare room, to my bed back home, maybe any bed anywhere. Now the door is ajar again.

I'm a girl who digs a chance
to get out on that floor and dance

Her room, if you enter, is just a neat, compartmental-
ized, one-windowed box with sections for books, for yard
goods, for notebooks, for keepsakes— but the first thing
you notice is the background odor, which is of perfume
mixed with stale cigarette smoke. That doesn't sound invit-
ing, but you might not turn and run.

> *I've danced in the east,*
> *I've danced in the west,*
> *and the thing that I like best is*

Enid once told me she was going to be a singer— that
was when one of her husband's friends, who instead be-
came a doctor, was going to be a songwriter. Do I think
Enid might get married again? Any such new husband
would certainly want the sofa cleared, or perhaps a new, less
comfortable sofa, and, simultaneously, the cats declawed.
That would all be too bad, but what do I have to do with it
outside of being a worrier about Enid? Now the bedroom
door is opening wide.

> *BOYS who do the BOP,*
> *MAN, they never STOP.*
> *Give 'em cut time*
> *and, man, they're flying,*
> *those BOYS who do the BOP*

Enid, wearing different pants, walks from her room to-
ward the bathroom.

> *those BOYS—Boys! Boys! Boys!*
> *who DO—do do do do do*
> *the BOP—Boys who bop!*

I'm no help, either. On Tuesday, after I came back and

told her about a girl I met over at the Peabody, Enid
stopped wearing a bra. She set up the ironing board right in
front of where I was typing and started ironing with her
shirt mostly open, so what did I do but ask how come she
usually wears a bra. She said something about gravity and
time, then left the room, and when she came back she'd but-
toned her shirt nearly up to her neck.

"Hullo, anybody home?" Enid, now through with bed-
room and bathroom, says to me, then turns her attention
to one of the cats. "What, not enough litter for a cute
thing to scratch? We call Cat Litter King, o.k.?" She picks
up the cat and brings its face to hers as she sits by the
phone and dials the King's message machine. "Greetings!
Enid and cats on Comm Ave. wouldn't mind a royal visit.
We want a case of cat food that says 'Cat Food.' Not with-
out labels, not cat-and-dog food, and not labeled 'Dog
Food' that you say is cat food. One hundred pounds of lit-
ter in ten-pound bags, not two fifties—what do you think
we are? We're home late tonight and all tomorrow night.
Sois prudent, Your Highness." What an entertainer! Enid is
no snob!

Enid puts down the phone and the cat, and is lost to me
for a few minutes. I think she is thinking about the past,
which is something I've pretty well cultivated out of myself,
thinking about the past. As I turn off the typewriter, Enid
looks over at me and says, "Let's go here, let's go there!
That's the thing to do, right?"

::

There was nothing like the Cat Litter King where I
came from; there were also things in Boston I couldn't get
used to. Just before I first visited Enid, her small white cat,
the one she told me would sleep on her neck, got stolen
from out front by the junkies down the block. "Let's go

get it back?" a friend of hers had mocked my suggestion. "Noonie, you don't go confronting addicts!" So as I went up and down Commonwealth Avenue putting up Lost Cat signs I had to fill my mind with other things, like memorizing the alphabetically ordered cross streets—Arlington, Exeter, Fairfax or Fairfield, Gloucester; that's all I remember now, and Exeter Street's easy, because that's where the Exeter Street Theatre was.

It was only a couple of days later that Enid started talking about my getting some kind of job, though following right up with how after she moved to Boston she'd go through the Help Wanteds, circle all the interesting ones, fold the newspaper neatly on top of her recycling pile, and then go out to a museum or two. Once Enid did get me something part time at Faneuil Hall Marketplace. She was working near there then, so a lot of times we got to have lunch together, and I even started thinking maybe that's why she got me the job. If it was a nice day and I got off early, I would go back to her place and sleep on the sofa in the sun with the cats. On days I wasn't working, I would walk and walk—one day I did the whole Freedom Trail—or just turn to my Old List, which was some basic things that had looked at first to me impossible to do but that just about everybody seemed able to do, like skipping rope, riding a bike, driving a car (or, as I updated the list, if you learned on an automatic, then driving a standard), swimming, and, of course, typing. (I don't have a New List but do keep an Auxiliary one, which is for not-impossible-looking things, like certain dances.)

::

Enid and I set out walking and, by the Charles River, Enid lights up a cigarette and tells me how her mother, who smokes, too, waits until everybody at their house has gone to bed and then goes outside on the patio and breathes out, all the way, emptying her lungs—push push push—completely, then breathes in a full load of fresh air, and then forces every bit out again, convinced that she's cleaning that day's smoking out of her lungs. I laugh at that, really laugh, and after a two-second delay Enid laughs, too.

I've never actually met Enid's mother, but I talked to her on the phone once when she called and Enid was out. She knew who I was and kept calling me by my first name, again and again, with the most luxurious voice. Enid has every right to sound like that but doesn't. Enid's mother wanted, I think, to ask me how Enid *really* was, and I wasn't so sure of myself that I said anything that would make her worry, but I didn't try to make her not worry, either.

Here, there; and from the Cambridge side of the Charles, up by MIT, Enid points out the narrow eastern face of the new Hancock building and tells me that it reflects the sunrise in a long vertical line, and that the western end does the same at sunset. (You've got to admire the Hancock, though it's tall and modern, and modern with problems. Try looking at it from the south when you're way down on Tremont, or from the north, from beside the old Hancock, going right up close.) "I liked it in plywood and I like it now —windows and all, as long as nobody gets hurt," Enid says, while reaching one hand over her head, tracing a halo's shape with her finger, around and around.

It isn't late when we get back to her place, but Enid's tired, and does have to get up early to move her car for Friday street-cleaning before going to work, so right away she puts on that white cotton nightdress of hers and gets into bed. I feel bad that we've developed any sort of routine at all, Enid and I, because soon I'm probably going to be someplace else, and, to take just one example, who's going to read from her book, that scrapbook of stories about sleep she's put together in her more-than thirty-one years? Every evening I've been reading something from it to her after she gets into bed. It's a great book—so good that I've had all three hundred and sixty-six oversize pages photo-copied to take with me when I go. Tonight's story was taken from the autobiography of Benjamin Franklin:

```
... I had walked again up the street, which by
this time had many clean-dressed people in it,
who were all walking the same way. I joined them
and thereby was led into the great meeting-house
of the Quakers near the market. I sat down among
them, and, after looking round awhile and hearing
nothing said, being very drowsy thro' labor and
want of rest the preceding night, I fell fast
asleep, and continued so till the meeting broke
up, when one was kind enough to rouse me. This
was, therefore, the first house I was in, or
slept in, in Philadelphia.
```

Philadelphia? I only have to hear a city's name and I start to get ideas. Actually, I'd kind of made up my mind to try New York.

"Enid?"

"What, Noo?"

"Are there any more words to the song?"

"There's more I can't remember right now. I think I'm asleep."

Before I leave this time I'm going to get those Bop lyrics on paper; otherwise I'll have to write to wherever she is, and what if she has a new last name?

"Is it o.k. if I stay up and type?"

"S'all right. I like a little background noise when I dream." (Enid really doesn't mind it when I stay up late and type.)

It was only ten-thirty and I still wasn't sleepy, so I started looking through the cupboards for something to eat. Next to three boxes of Wheatena and behind the saltines was an open bag of Pepperidge Farm Tahiti cookies. There were only two cookies in the bag, and since I hate to eat the last of anything when there's someone else who might come snacking, I took just one cookie. Then, maybe because I was alone and it seemed so quiet, I got out a pen and wrote in ink on the bag, "Contains One Only—No Good if You're Hungry." I put the bag back on the shelf, went and stretched out on the sofa, and thought some more about Benjamin Franklin, and then Thomas Jefferson, and then John Hancock, and then whether or not I'd kissed Enid good night. I had, but it was the kind of kiss you can't expect to go far, a kiss without plans.

::

So all that was a Thursday night. Then Friday, then Saturday, then Sunday; then Monday I left for New York, and I haven't seen Enid since. I did leave her my P.O. box address from back home, because I wasn't sure where I'd end up, and my cousin who works at the post office is good about forwarding things. Using that system, I've received three communications from Enid, three in five years:

1. In a puffy envelope mailed not long after I left Boston was the empty Pepperidge Farm cookie bag, with an "N" added to my note; i.e., "Contains NOne Only—No Good if You're Hungry."

2. Several months after that I received a postcard showing the lobby of a hotel in a place like Tahiti, and there, among other words, was "honeymoon"—not as in "Hoyle Up-to-Date," not honeymoon bridge. (Enid once told me that her mother used to tell her, "You might as well be nice." Even with that I couldn't decide whether or not to send a wedding present, which is to say I didn't.)

3. Then nothing for over four years until this menu, here in my hand, reached me earlier today. No message, but each dish and price printed in Enid's hand, along with the restaurant's name, and its address, three thousand miles away. I looked at the menu for a long time, and did think of writing something on it like "Menu Only—No Good if You're Hungry" and sending it back, but then thought better of it. (Another thing I'd been cultivating was thinking better of things.)

As for what went the other way, once in a while I'd sent her funny newspaper clippings and stuff, but every time I wrote a real letter I knew it was a mistake the minute I dropped it into the big blue box. And telephones? You can't get them to work right.

::

That's still a great song, that Bop one. It's a good thing I wrote down the words before leaving, but just getting lyrics on paper is not really how such things should be done. The way to make a song yours is by singing it—right? Some how-to-do book must say that. I gave my typing one away, because learning was so hard for me I began to feel that if I ever got good at it it would be while getting less good at something else.

Doing all right in New York, with all my books in one place for the first time in fourteen years, including two big identical old Random House dictionaries. I keep one at each end of my apartment so there's no lugging around. I turn to them often. "Menu" comes from the French for "detailed list," "detailed" as in "small and detailed," while "snob" has no accepted etymological origin—though I've heard of Latin teachers who like to say it's short for "Sine NOBili-tate", "without nobility." But Enid was no snob!

Enid's sofa was comfortable, yes, but on that Thursday night there was some noise from the street, a car radio play-ing loud, I think, so I moved my blankets into the spare room in back, which shared a wall with Enid's and was its mirror image. Unfortunately, the bed there was much too soft, and I still couldn't sleep. I started wondering if there was any part of a moon out that night, and if the long nar-row ends of the Hancock ever reflect moonlight in a line— if not when the moon is large but pale on the rise, then maybe when it's small and bright in the sky. A little while later I heard Enid get up, use the bathroom, and, I thought, go back to bed.

A few more minutes passed and then, from outside the spare-room window, came a sound that should have made me think of death, or birth, but even before I got up to look I knew what it was: Enid, expelling a day's intake from her almost thirty-two-year-old lungs, cleansing them well with the damp, night-morning air.

FATHER MUST

The question he asked me didn't start with "Father" or anything like that—I'm not his father. It wasn't the words in his question that made me think of the question I'd once asked my father.

The kid's a good kid. He's full of good questions. And while it's true that I haven't let him call me anything, that doesn't stop us from talking.

I did, different times, consider all the names he might call me, like Father or Papa or Daddy, but none ever seemed right. I could have let him call me by the name his mother and others do, but since I really don't care for it, that would miss the whole point.

I just once, early on, asked about the father, and she said it had been only one night; then, smiling and pretty, she said it gets dark at night. She said it takes more time than she took to know how a person really looks, so it was a very good thing that the kid looked like her.

When I'm with the kid and someone says he must look like his mother, I just say, "O.k." I don't say, "He's not only her." I don't say, "She's the one who had him, and now, mostly, I have him." I don't say, "She says that even though I don't let him call me anything she thinks that he likes me."

::

It's a nice place, this place; in the day, it has very good light. It's the same place that it was when she first brought me here—same full cupboards, same clean table. I did paint the ceilings, but everything else is the same, except for a few things now that are mine and more stuff that's the kid's.

By the way, I do like him, and it's not just because he's not my own age. When we go out for a walk—well, at first he was two in that red-and-blue stroller—I always ask him about something, because after he answers, and it's always a good answer, I like to ask anyway, "Now, are you sure?" I do it just to see that firm way he nods yes, and when I nod back, that dreamy look he gets because he likes being sure.

::

Billy Blair's my own age. He was my best friend in sixth grade, but now I don't see him often. The last time I did, I asked, "Hey, Billy Boy, does your mother still sing?" He said his mother never sang, and that's a bad answer, so I said, "But she did. When she was folding the wash, she would sing." And then, you know, he said something, and I didn't say back to him how maybe I was a drunk now but that I was just a plain pure boy in sixth grade when his mother sang.

Should I find a good doctor, or go to the meetings, meet people? I'd rather—really, I'd like to—go see Mrs. Blair. She's not my own age, so the question would work fine, and she'd even call me Jacksie, my name to people from then.

What if I was the only boy who ever noticed her singing? What I mean is not just the only boy but only man. (Someone should tell her. She really could sing.)

::

Of course, I'm not going to see Mrs. Blair. From the Blairs' house you can see my old house—diagonally across the street, on the next block, the house without trees. Well, there might be trees there now; it's been twenty years. My father wouldn't plant trees around the house. He said trees around a house get big by making the house small.

Did my mother like trees?

I'm not saying my father was wrong; I know what he meant, and what that meant, but it would have been nice to have trees.

::

Am I thinking of my father because of Billy Blair's answer, or because of the kid's question, or because today's Sunday? Just because the sun's not up yet doesn't mean it isn't Sunday. I'm here in the kitchen, drinking black coffee.

In Japan, there are now big factories that operate all night without lights—robots don't need lights. These factories of robots are dark in the dark; all black in black. You can hear these factories long before you can see them; you can be almost next to them and still not see them; you might have to touch them to see them.

::

I don't know why, but on Sunday mornings my father never got drunk. It wasn't because the liquor store wasn't open—he'd buy his week's supply on Saturdays. And it wasn't because he was religious. He used to say, "Don't tell anybody, but I've got some different angles on the cross." Maybe that's part of an old joke, I don't know. My father also used to say something else like that, but he'd recite it like poetry: There's only one God / God sees the little sparrow fall / There's only one God / He's for sparrows.

I never went to Sunday school, because my father, who wore suits and ties, didn't want to see me wearing suits and ties.

::

The sky, except for a few stars, is still dark. The moon has gone down without waiting for the sun to come up.

I was only thirteen when my mother died in the spring. I still think that spring is a strange time for someone to die. It was about noon when the people came back to the house from the funeral. My father came charging through a crowd of them shouting, "Take off that tie! Go to your room and change out of that suit!" That day wasn't a Sunday, but it was like a Sunday. I don't care what everyone thought, he hadn't been drinking that morning; he wasn't drunk, he was wild.

My father didn't last long—four-and-a-half years isn't long. I wore a suit and tie at his funeral and I thought, and people said, that I looked pretty good.

::

They let me stay in my house while I finished twelfth grade. I just wasn't supposed to be alone, although it turned out that a lot of the time I was. When anyone was staying in the house with me, I would sleep in my room, but when nobody was I'd move out into the den and sleep on the rug between lots of blankets.

A housekeeper would come in from ten until two five days a week, so I'd come home for lunch and when I'd finished eating she'd pour herself and me fresh coffee. I'd never liked coffee before. Because she hadn't known my parents, we talked about just anything while she mostly kept moving around the kitchen. When the housekeeper did sit, it was in my mother's chair. The housekeeper didn't know whose chair it had been, and I didn't mention it.

I was o.k. for money and had accounts at some places.

When I had to go to a doctor or dentist or something, I'd take a taxi. The first snowy day that winter, I got a driver who had just moved from China and had never seen snow before. I remember now that he kept saying, "So white. So beautiful." over and over again. Although he didn't speak English very well, he had a way of making the word "white" sound white and the word "beautiful" sound beautiful.

On Saturdays, the housekeeper would come for just two hours in the morning, so weekends were pretty quiet. Sundays were really quiet.

After the house was sold for me, I never went back there.

::

I'd been thinking again lately if I should let the kid call me something. If it doesn't work out between his mother and me, and I leave, he should be able to call me by a name if he sees me somewhere. I'd have no reason not to let him, and, who knows, sometime he might want to introduce me to someone.

If he called me by the name I'm called now, I still wouldn't like it, and especially not from him, because the name was my father's, so I'd been thinking, Why not Jacksie or Jacks? Until yesterday, I'd pretty much settled on Jacks, which was what people called me when I lived alone in the house.

If I let him just once call me something, I was thinking, then it would be up to him—he's almost seven—whether or not to call me that from then on. But then I thought should I let him start calling me something right away or wait to see how things work out with his mother and me?

::

It might not seem easy to breathe any love into a name like Father. It's a stiff word—it's not soft, like, say, Papa—but sometimes you have to breathe love into names you don't choose.

Yesterday, Saturday, in the afternoon, the kid had a question he came in the house to ask me, and the question didn't start with "Father" or anything like that—he knows I'm not his father—and there was nothing like "must" in his question. (As the sun comes up, this kitchen will get brighter; the ceiling, the table, the cupboards are white.)

The kid's question was just one about a picture on the box the Wiffle ball come in, which shows the curve and the slider, but because he was looking lower than my eyes, at the bottle I'd just opened, it made me think of the question I'd once asked my father, who I called Father.

It's only now that I'm thinking that my father might have heard my question before, not from being asked but by asking, and the answer he might have been given could have been the same one he, a glass at his lips, gave me.

When the kid asked me his question yesterday about the curve and the slider, what he wanted was for me to come outside and catch the ball for him, and throw it to him. He wanted to watch his own throw and see mine, and then talk it over, so he could be sure.

So I went outside with him and the Wiffle ball, but first I used the same answer I'd been given to a different question. Now the kid can call me that or not that, whatever he likes; he doesn't have to worry. And I know that he heard me—he looked up at my eyes when I said, "Father must."

SATELLITE DISH

If you think it's too cold for a woman my age to be eating her lunch out here by the beaver dam, then the first thing I have to tell you is, don't worry about me. Or, if I say it the way I first said it as a little girl, "Don't worry 'bout me."

I seem to have been saying and thinking the same things right from the beginning. For a long time my mother would look at me as if the things I was saying were a little bit funny—just a little bit, not funny enough one way to laugh at or the other way to get upset about.

I don't know—is "Don't worry 'bout me" such a funny thing to say if you're a small child? Many times after I'd said it my mother would ask me if I was angry about anything. I told her I didn't think so. Maybe what I should have said to her was that I just didn't like to have anyone worrying about me. But I don't know if I knew that yet. After a while my mother didn't say any more about it, but she would still sometimes look at me closely when I said it, as if she were looking not just into my eyes but into my whole face, if that's possible.

I did start to wonder once if it might have something to do with the trains that used to go by our house—if the things I was thinking and saying might be funny because whenever I asked anyone a question I didn't hear the answer right because just then a train went by.

This is nice and hot, this vegetable soup. I make it with celery, onions, and carrots. Fresh tomato for base. The sandwich I baked the bread for in the wood stove. Now, it might look like that's roast beef in the sandwich, but it's really a thin-sliced leftover from last night. We had steak, with green beans and mashed potatoes, and then apple pie for dessert. I could have brought some apple pie with me today, but there was this nice little piece of angel-food cake.

It wasn't so cold yesterday, but I didn't take my usual walk out here. A rather cheerless day, yesterday. Maybe just because it's the end of the season. Couldn't interest myself in anything—not knitting, not reading, not anything—so I just crawled into bed with my thoughts.

Just as one thing I say is "Don't worry about me," one thing I think is that you love somebody by living with them. Now my husband—maybe he lived with me because I loved him, and even maybe he lived with me because he loved me, but he never loved me by living with me. Anyway, I was married once, long ago. Three children, two now away.

The satellite dish up by the barn, next to the road, on this side? Hard to miss it. My son, his wife, and the boys watch programs from all over the world now. I really do like living in my own home with family about, yet often when I hear them talking and I think it has to do with people around here but the names aren't familiar and I ask, it turns out to be about something that was on TV. So I do miss out on some talk that way, because I really don't look at the television too often. And if I haven't much interesting to say sometimes, maybe that's why.

This bread of mine, I think it's very tasty. It's from my grandmother's recipe, though I never knew her. But I do make it like my mother did, not only by the recipe but from having watched her. So it should be the same. And I've started using the wood stove again. So now it's exactly the same.

They say you shouldn't slice bread hot, but my mother would, for me. And now, if anyone's interested, I offer to do it for them. And I do it for myself, too. Because it's always the same for me, that fresh hot bread.

The pond here, that's something that's not the same. More like a lake now. Up at the other end, it's still as good for wading as it used to be, but most times now I'll just sit down at this end and watch the water trickling over the beaver dam. When it's warm enough, I dangle my feet in. And I saw lots of baby beavers this summer—so cute.

Do you think people change? Maybe it's that they appear to —if they really do, I don't know. If it's a sudden change, maybe it's just that they go back to being like they really were all along. If it's a slow change, as they grow older, it's probably just them becoming more like they are—I think people don't get less like they are; they get more like they are. Sometimes the change is toward you. But sometimes it's away. Even if they love you. Even if you love them by living with them.

I like a crusty bread. Last spring, when the man who sold my son the satellite dish told him that the signal wasn't coming in good because of the big old elm tree across the road by the house, that it was getting in the way of the reception, everyone—my son, my daughter-in-law, my grandsons, and then, because everyone else was, even the man—looked at me. I loved that tree. It was always there. It would always make me feel good to walk in the yard through its patterned shadow on my way into the house. But then, across the road, there was the satellite dish. I said they could chop down the tree, but that I wanted every bit of wood from it cut and stacked in a pile by itself. And though I hadn't done it for years, since we'd got an electric stove and a furnace, I started back using the old wood stove, which we'd left in the kitchen mostly for looks. It's better to cook bread in a wood stove anyway. You can tell the difference not just in the crust but also in taste.

That elm tree was healthy. Perfect. Solid all the way through. So at least I'm putting it to good use. Even with such a warm summer I did. And I will, until that wood's used up.

Anyway, it's something else to keep me occupied. I do like a full day. That way, when night comes I'm tired, and can fall asleep fast. Then morning comes quick. After breakfast, that's when I take my walk down behind the house where the trains used to run. Since they took up the tracks, it's left a nice path. I almost always see rabbits.

::

The trains weren't really a good explanation for all those things I was thinking and saying back then and for all these years now, because the trains went by only four times a day, and one of those times I was usually in school and you could hardly hear the train from the school. And two more times I'd be in bed—for the late-night train, I'd be asleep, or almost asleep, and for the early-morning train I'd be just waking up. So unless I was dreaming and asking questions and getting answers in my dreams, and with just one other time of day when the train went by, the things I've always been thinking and saying couldn't have had much to do with those trains. And you know, at night, if I think about it, I start to miss the sound of the trains.

What I will miss now, until spring, is people coming up from the city for vegetables and things. Sometimes you meet people who, even though you never saw them before, when you talk to them it's as if they're answering questions inside of you that you don't even ask. People like that I start thinking I could live with.

Some things have happened in my life and some haven't. And I always got along by going carefully—that's even how I have to walk now. But you see a little light and you scratch at it. For a little more light. That's what I do. If you find life a little dark, I think that's what to do. Even if it only amounts to making tea for someone and serving cookies. Any little things I might do to get a little more light—well, I'm not ashamed to do them.

Could be an early cold winter. The moon was getting nice and round last night, so there might be a frost soon. I should cover the tomatoes. I wonder if anyone will remember that I like to take my own apples down to the cider mill to get pressed. Won't make any plans, but I love to go.

Didn't get enough beets this year—enough to eat, but not enough to pickle. Next year, more beets, and maybe more Swiss chard, too. And some flowers closer to the house.

The angel food's gone, so I'll get on my way. You know, whenever I cross the road now, even if I'm looking down just at my feet, I can feel the satellite dish above and behind me where it wasn't before, and the tree and its shadow not above and ahead of me where they were before. All those things seem to make me walk differently—not slower but stiffer.

How would it all look to you after I walked from the beaver dam here, through the field? Up by the road, as you drove over the rise? On the left you'd see the barn, then the satellite dish, then me—don't worry 'bout me—crossing the line in the road on my way to the yard and the house on the right. But you wouldn't see a patterned shadow of the tree on the house and the yard, and you wouldn't see the tree.

ELEVATOR NEIGHBORS

The first time Jane saw Bim, she and I were standing at the table near the elevator, checking the mail. About a week, say, after I signed the latest lease. So for her, living here with me, that would have been a few days in.

I turned my head and raised my hand to wave, but Bim didn't see us because he walked out of the elevator looking straight ahead, going right outside—on his way, I suppose to the grocery store.

When we got into the elevator and the doors closed, Jane asked, "So who's your friend?"

I said, "He's not so much a friend; he lives on five."

"Just him?"

"He's taken."

"But...," she said, smiling. "So were you."

I like the way it goes with Jane. I don't have to lie—I've never lied to her. And I don't have to tell the exact truth—that Bim's really, really taken. That it has to do with how he gets his information. So I just said, "Bim's not me," with the elevator rising.

::

Bim, almost any afternoon, down at the grocery store on the corner, buying tangerines: testing them between his thumb and fingers, deciding in his palm. One hand selects as many as the other hand can hold—three tangerines, or four, or five, depending on the size. He pays and steps out onto the sidewalk. Sliding the hand with the tangerines into his jacket pocket, he releases all but one: that tangerine, both hands help to peel. Then it's his selecting hand that separates a section and brings it to his lips as he walks away to work.

It's not that I follow Bim around all day, or spend much time thinking about what Bim does or why he does it, but since he lives on the floor below me I can't help seeing him a lot. And sometimes in the elevator, though Bim's not there, I'll see a tangerine that I figure must have fallen from his pocket when he was taking out his keys. I like tangerines o.k., so when this happens I pick it up, and as I walk along I peel and eat it—nothing special, at least not for me. I mean, I don't know what it is with Bim and tangerines, but it must be something.

Bim and Lily, they're on five and I'm on six. All the other tenants hate us because of the elevator thing. They call us the Elevator Neighbors, but it was the landlord, down on one, who set up this system, long before any of us moved in. When he converted this building from a factory, instead of installing a new elevator he just fixed the old one; then, thinking that with less use it might last longer, he sealed the elevator entrances to two, three, and four. He left our floors alone: good fifth- and sixth-floor-walkup tenants might not be easy to find and keep. (If anyone downstairs from us complains to him, he says that according to the law this building doesn't have to have an elevator at all.)

For a while, Bim and Lily tried letting the other tenants take heavy things up on the elevator into their place and then out and down the stairs, but it usually ended up being just as hard to move stuff down the stairs as up. And if anyone says anything to me about the elevator I just put it this way: "You think I like the landlord?"

I *do* like the landlord—him with his one-year leases, always thinking that the city's going to let the controls on rents expire. Then, with one-year leases, he wouldn't have to wait longer to raise the rents. But I like a one-year lease as opposed to a two-year lease, because then I never have to stop and think if it's the year to sign a new lease or not. And because I always look forward to the day I sign the lease, a one-year lease is twice as good as a two-year lease to me.

::

Bim and I moved into our floors at the same time. Bim alone, really alone, unlike me—I was just waiting to get settled before asking Sandra to move in.

The landlord actually gave Bim and me the same appointment to sign our leases. So that's where I first met Bim, in the landlord's office. There we were, both painters needing space to live and paint, signing leases with identical terms.

After shaking hands with the landlord, Bim and I went out and had a burger. Bim told me he worked five nights a week as a dinner chef and I felt bad to have to tell him that I'd started painting full-time. But Bim already knew my work, because I was beginning to get shown in some galleries here and there. I hadn't seen any of Bim's paintings then, but I had a feeling that they were probably not much like mine, because when I told him I used mostly acrylic paints he said he used all oils.

::

It was five one-year leases ago, about six months in, at three in the morning, when Sandra woke me up, all worried. At first I thought it was smoke, because the air seemed heavy, but as I started to get more wide-awake I said to Sandra,

"That's turpentine. I don't use it, but Bim might—he paints with oils." Though so much that it would come up through the floorboards? And in the middle of the night?

I pulled on some clothes, ran down the stairs to Bim's place, and knocked on the door: "You awake, Bim?" It wasn't long before Bim opened the door, a finger on his lips.

"I am, but *she's* not," he said, pointing over at the sofa. With the paintbrush in his other hand he motioned me in.

"So everything's o.k.? Sandra and I were wondering about the turpentine. We never noticed it before."

"Never painted all night before," said Bim, and I followed his eyes to a painting at the other end of the room, and then back to the sofa. Whoever she was, sleeping there in a sweatshirt and jeans, partly covered by a mohair blanket, she looked familiar.

"You don't know Lily?" he said. "You eat breakfast every day where she works."

But I didn't know her name, because she's second shift there, and I go in early. "Yeah," I said. "I see her coming in, having coffee with the busboys at the back before she starts."

"Ten to four-thirty. When I was having lunch in there today, I told her that if she'd come over to the place where I cook, I'd feed her dinner in the kitchen. So she comes straight from work and stays, watching, eating a little bit of this, of that—stays until I'm through. And then she says, 'Now that I've tasted your cooking, I want to see your painting.' So I brought her back here and dragged out a few paintings and she says, 'No, not your paintings. Your painting. You painting.' So she goes and stretches out on the sofa, and I start painting with her watching. Around midnight she falls asleep. So I just cover her up and then keep painting."

I looked again at Lily sleeping, and then the other way, at the painting Bim was working on. I couldn't tell if what I was seeing was because of the lights Bim was using or if it was a way Bim had of painting light. "Bim," I said. "You buy some kind of special lights?"

"Nope," said Bim. "Just plain old lights."

I stayed a few more minutes. When I got back upstairs, Sandra asked me, "Turpentine?"

"Turpentine," I said.

And then she asked, "So what's going on down there?"

Later I thought about it—if what I answered was actually lying, because what could I really say about painting light like that, or painting all night, if I'd never done it? I suppose it would have been true to say, "Bim painting, Lily sleeping." But then Sandra would have asked me who *Lily* was. I mean, if you're introduced to someone when she's sleeping, what can you say about her? That she's just some waitress? That wouldn't sound right. So because of all that I lied. And because I'd never lied to her before, she didn't notice that first time.

So, sure, I knew I was lying when I said to Sandra, "Nothing."

::

The morning after I met Lily, when I went for breakfast where she works I asked Karen, the waitress there who I'd known the longest, "Besides working here, what's Lily do?"

"Who knows? She never talks about anything like that."

"Do you think she paints?"

"Her face, a little. But don't you find her kind of bony?"

"Look, I just met her downstairs in my building last night."

"Then why didn't you ask her yourself?"

"I never like to ask—anyway, she was asleep."

"Then you should have asked Bim."

"You know Bim?"

"I *knew* Bim."

"O.k.," I said. "So maybe you don't like Lily."

"What I know about her is that she looks like her father."

"You know her father?"

"She was going through her wallet one day and I asked her about a picture in it and she said it was her father. Same nice facial structure. Same eyebrows, same color hair. Then I started to wonder if I didn't know that anyway. Sometimes without ever seeing the mother or father you can tell which one the daughter looks like. And one more thing...." Then Karen surprised me. "Except for her moving a little too fast —in here, on her feet, got that? Making me look slow? I really don't mind Lily."

::

After Lily moved in with Bim, the turpentine at night became a regular thing. Sandra wasn't bothered by it—things didn't seem to bother her when she knew what they were. But whenever I suggested to her that we invite Bim and Lily up she said she spent enough time, at the gallery where she worked, with artists who were cooks and, in restaurants where she ate, with waitresses who might or might not be artists. Me, I was becoming much less interested in just what else, if anything, Lily did, or whether Bim's painting would ever be in demand. I began to think that riding in the elevator with Bim and Lily, or either one of them, or even one of Bim's tangerines, might be one of the nicer things that could happen to me in a day. And maybe one of the nicer things that happened in a year was when I'd set up the lease-signing appointment on one of Bim's days off. After signing, Bim and I would go from the landlord's office to meet Lily after work and the three of us would go and have a burger somewhere. Once, just once, I also got Sandra to meet us, but I ended up spending so much time trying to keep her from asking Lily *exactly* what it is she does, or had ever done, or planned to do, that I really lost the evening. And that made it like having a two-year lease.

Other than lease-signing days, the longest time I ever spent with Bim alone was when I drove him out to catch a plane when his mom got sick. As we walked through the airport, it seemed to me that every woman in the place was looking at us. But whenever I looked back at any of them I noticed that the angle of the gaze was never quite right, their eyes not meeting mine. A little higher, a little to the side—it was just Bim they were looking at. And there was Bim, looking only straight ahead, always seeming to take too much time before brushing the hair out of his eyes.

I almost walked right by him once because of the way he lets that hair just fall over his face. On days when I used to meet Sandra at work uptown, I'd go a little early and see what was doing at the Met. And I was walking up the steps outside when this hand with a tangerine pushes out at me. There's Bim, sitting, elbows on his knees.

"Hey," I said. "Any good shows in there?"

Bim, peeling the tangerine and handing me half: "I just came up to see a painting,"

"Just one?"

I sat down and he told me which one, and he had to tell me where, because it was a painting I was only slightly familiar with. And nothing at all like anything that I or, I thought then, Bim would paint.

As I got up, I said, "Lease time's coming around."

"O.k. Set it up," said Bim, bringing a section of tangerine to his lips.

When I got inside the museum, the first thing I went to, of course, was that painting. No, nothing like what either Bim or I would paint, not what's in it. But then I found myself trying to figure out the lighting in the room—until I remembered the last time I'd done that. And just like then, in Bim's place, it wasn't the room that was strangely lit.

::

I'd always been so careful not to ask Lily questions that in almost four years I'd hardly talked to her at all. Over the yearly lease-signing burgers, she'd mostly just listen to Bim and me. In the elevator it would be things like the weather, or I would just say hi when I saw her walking double-speed into work in the mornings, or just as fast afterward to hang around where Bim was cooking. With Bim, on her days off, Lily had another, almost sideways way of walking: slower, and she'd face into him and talk and talk and talk. And he'd be walking, looking straight ahead, as usual, but nodding his head and smiling. I used to try to avoid them when I saw them like that, because I didn't want to interrupt. Then one time—it was just before Sandra left—they were walking and saw me and stopped to say hello. After a bit, I noticed Lily looking at my jacket—I was wearing an old khaki jacket. "Something you like about my jacket, Lily?" I guess that's the first question I'd ever asked her.

"Yes," she said. "It...." Then she turned to Bim and said, as if I weren't there, "It softens him." And then, because I was there, she turned back to me. "It softens you."

::

I'd started spending time with Jane just before Sandra moved out. It was about halfway between leases, and I thought, Let's see what happens. Let's wait six months—I can work here but sleep at Jane's place. And see if I feel I won't start lying as I lied to Sandra through all those one-year leases, starting with the first one, six months in. So even after Sandra left, it was a while before Jane moved in here with me.

I'd almost decided to give up this place, because I really

should be thinking about buying something of my own. But when lease-signing time was coming around and Bim, as he did every year, said, "Set it up." I thought I might as well stay put for now.

The morning of the day we were going to sign the lease, I was sitting in the restaurant when Lily came in. I started thinking that, with Sandra gone, and with Jane still at her place and busy packing, instead of going out somewhere afterward why not take Bim and Lily back to my place, because they'd never been there. Rent a movie. Cook up something. And later I'd go over to Jane's.

I went to the back of the restaurant, where Lily was drinking coffee and listening to the busboys. When I told her my idea, she said they had some food that Bim had brought home from work the night before, and it could be a kind of picnic, but then she said, "Maybe hold off on the movie. Because Bim might not like a movie."

I said, "Bim and I could drop by the video place before we pick you up here. He could choose it."

"But he couldn't choose the frames."

"He...."

"Bim finds movies too full of things to see."

"Oh."

"Bim's very careful how he gets his information."

I was trying to think of something to say to make myself more comfortable. "Ted Williams," I said. "Ted Williams played baseball for the—"

"The Boston Red Sox," said Lily.

"Right, the Boston Red Sox. Ted Williams, when he was playing for the Red Sox, never saw a movie because he wanted to save his eyes for seeing the pitch." I looked at Lily. "But that's different."

Lily thought for a minute as she started to get ready for her shift. "Um, different, different, but not so different."

That night, after we'd finished eating and I was leaving to

go to Jane's, I said, "Come on," and pointed to the elevator. "I'll let you out at your place. How often in this building do you get to take the elevator one floor down?"

At five, I kept my hand on the button that holds the door open. I said to Bim, "Hey this morning Lily was filling me in on Ted Williams and the Red Sox...."

Lily started laughing. She said, "My father must have thought I was the closest thing to a boy in our family. He wouldn't stop talking to me. And I loved to listen."

There'd be no one waiting to use the elevator. I kept my hand on the button and allowed myself a question. "So there's more like you at home, Lily?"

Lily looked at Bim.

"He wants to know about your *sisters*, Lily."

"Oh. Well, there's two of them, but they're really not so much like me. They're... they're like...."

"They're like *each other*," said Bim to Lily. And then he said it again, but to me. "They're like *each other*."

I used the hand that was holding the button to wave good night.

::

Anyway, it's late. Already, some nights, three months in, this happens.

"It's late," says Jane. "Honey, come to bed."

I turn off the VCR and in the dark, with open eyes, I get in bed. My hands know where I am and where they are, and you would think that whatever I'm then becoming part of would be enough to set aside that turpentine.

But that turpentine—if it starts to float up through the floorboards, I guess I start to float inside of it. Because the next thing I know, Jane has to say my name—my name, but as a question. And, so far, that's the only question that she asks, because, by asking it, I'm back.

But what happens if Jane starts asking *more* than that? Not just in bed, but other times, when something makes me think of Bim painting light with Lily sleeping. Or Bim and tangerines. Or my khaki jacket. Sandra used to ask.

If Jane starts asking? I'll start lying. I'll say, "Nothing." If it's something.

READ CHINESE

Still sleeping? Or just not out of bed yet? I wasn't gone long. You know, you can—you'll say you can't, but you can —read Chinese. Maybe not a book, but for sure a newspaper. In any language, a newspaper's a newspaper. You look at it, you turn the pages—you can tell which parts are the news and which parts are the ads. You can look at the photographs, the drawings, the border designs. You can figure out what's international, what's local, what's fashion, what's entertainment, what's sports, what's business. Some of the words you can read because some of them they don't translate. Some people's names they don't translate. So you have a bunch of Chinese characters and then you have a name like ROY ORBISON. Yesterday there was an article that was all Chinese characters except for ROY ORBISON six times. So most names they go ahead and translate, but others they don't. And K-MART they don't translate. And THE SUNSHINE STATE they don't translate. Certain expressions they don't translate—KEEP FIT they don't translate. BYE-BYE they don't translate. Some words you think they would they don't translate. DOWNTOWN they don't translate. And SPAGHETTI and PASTA they don't translate.

::

That's Chinese newspapers, but spoken Chinese—sometimes in the coffee and pastry shops here in Chinatown I mimic the words I hear, but very softly. If you do it, don't get too loud, because then it sounds like an echo, and people start looking around.

Chinese, spoken, is such a pleasing language. So many tones—it's like singing. Since I don't know what I'm saying, I never try to use those words when it comes my turn to order. I say, "One of those, one of those, one of those, one of those, and one of those. And one of those." All in one tone. Not so pleasing.

::

Oh, you learn a few things in Chinatown. One thing is that you don't whistle. Because whistling in China is what the blind people there, the ones who massaged for a living, would do as they walked down the alleyways. Like the ice-cream man here, but whistling, not bells. And parents would send their children out to the alleyway to put their hands on the walking sticks of the blind people to guide them into the houses that needed their touch.

And in restaurants you learn. For instance, it means something if you're alone and order bird's-nest soup and the waiter smiles and says, "Good for you." If he tells you what it means when you're alone and you order it, you might change your mind on the soup, but some of the things he says you'll remember exactly: "And if you live in a house full of love you love the house. You love the bird that builds its nest under the eaves of the house."

Do you have anything you want washed? The laundromat I leave my stuff at uses a Chinese kind of soap; maybe you noticed. When I'm in another part of town and I want to calm down, I just go and sit by myself somewhere. I don't actually shut my eyes—I just keep still until I can smell the soap in my shirt.

::

Who knows, who knows how it will go? What you want, what I want, and so on. The Chinese seem to have fewer words than we do. Maybe they make every three words into two—so one word would cover "want" and "desire," and one would cover "desire" and "need." Roy Orbison, Roy Orbison, Roy Orbison, Roy Orbison, Roy Orbison, Roy Orbison—right now that's all I can say.

Are you sure you're awake? Don't you like mornings? But it's o.k. for you to keep sleeping while I go out and come back like this. What's great about living in Chinatown is that there's so many people getting up in the morning knowing what they want that I start wanting what they want. So this is coffee with cream and sugar. That's right, cream and sugar —don't you want to try some things that I like? I tried some things that you like. Some of them I liked. These are sweet rolls, all different kinds.

And because I know that the world really doesn't—at least not for long—go away, I picked up some newspapers. Three published here, two from Hong Kong. Let's see... here, you start with this one. It's in—they all are, and now that you know you can, you can read—Chinese.

COUSIN

Cousin, you're a rough diamond—you're diamond-hard, hard to follow. Even for me it's not easy to keep up. Sometimes you go slow, so you don't lose me completely; sometimes when I act like I almost want to get lost, you drop back to get me; and even though you're always letting me know, again and again, that I'm closest to you, and most like you—Cousin, even with all that, I barely understand what you say and do.

How did it go last night when I came over to your house and wanted to watch the news on TV? You said, "Maybe not tonight. Come on, I'll show you a good place to watch the sun set." So we got in my car and I drove where you told me, up one paved road, and one dirt one, and then, because my car was too low to get through, we got out and walked up an old logging road until we came to a clearing where there was a stand of trees, mostly birch.

"Now, Cousin," you said. "I heard somewhere that on the night of the full moon in July the birch trees give up their bark. It's just like the tides." You talked about how it all comes together—the time of the year, the pull of the moon, the warmth in the air, the wet in the trees—and said that when the moon was high, if I just touched the bark it would fall into my hands. And then you said, "I'd stay here myself, Cousin, but my son wants something to drive tonight—and you know those trucks. I'd give him my car, but the wife should have that. So you stay here, and then he can use your car."

"You want me to stay here all night?" I said.

"Besides, my wife wouldn't sleep well if I were out in the woods," you said. "You, Cousin, you're perfect for this. You, no one will miss."

Cousin, you're like life, you are *rough*. Then, as you walked away, though all I could think of was your son with my car, what I yelled after you was "I'm supposed to spend the night out here doing that? And how can removing the bark be good for the trees?"

And you, still walking, said, "It is not so much that you *remove* as...."

And then I couldn't tell what you said, so I called out, "What did you say?" And I guess you said it again, but you were farther away, so I still couldn't make out that last word.

You must have stopped and turned around long enough to shout back one more thing, because I did hear you say, "And not now. You have to wait for the moon."

::

Six trucks, Cousin, and not one of them working right. The Chev with no muffler. The red Dodge that won't start and the blue one that won't stop. The Japanese thing you can see through. The Ford—all right, I found you that Ford, but you agreed, so we both can be wrong on old Fords. And that jeep-style heap—good engine, but not much of a transmission left to get power to the wheels, so, because the tires were good, we put the wheels on the Chev.

Cousin, you want what you want from me and you know how to get it. Like last night, you must have known that hearing about tides in the trees would be something I'd like. But that other time, when I really wanted something from you—I'm not saying I didn't get it, but, since you have your own ways, you weren't easy to follow.

"Just because you want to talk about her doesn't mean we're going to," you said. And I would have left it at that, for a while, anyway, but then you said, "We could go see her stone." Somehow I'd never seen it. It was a hundred miles inland and I'd always stayed around home whenever anyone else went. So we got in one of the trucks that were working then, but at the end of the driveway did you turn left to go inland? You didn't say anything, and did I say one word as you turned right to drive the other way, toward the shore? First down a paved road, then a dirt one, and then, where I was sure that all the roads ended, we took an old hauling road the fishermen used.

When we stopped and got out, I noticed that, although there wasn't much of a beach, there were some big, sharp, dark rocks at the high-water mark that sheltered some larger, light, rounded, smooth ones on the land. Even with a storm out at sea those sharp rocks would take all the force of the waves that came in, and keep the smooth ones mostly dry. I saw right away that, if you wanted to, you could lean into those smooth rocks, or up against them, and be held half standing as you slept in the sun. Those smooth rocks there, surrounded by sparse grass growing up through the sand, were the ones you walked toward and around, Cousin, looking at each of them until one stopped you. You ran your hand over it and said, "Here it is. This is it. This is the one." Then you showed me a heart shape that had been carved into it, with your sister's initials and someone else's and the year inside.

"O.k., Cousin, I get it," I said. "A rock is a stone. But that year is before my time and kind of early in yours—whose initials are those with hers?"

"Just some local guy she was seeing."

"So they'd come here, like on picnics?"

"Cousin. Cousin. They'd come here at night."

And then, as I looked at that large smooth rock and its angle, I was wondering whether she'd been heaven or earth, her back against the sky or the rock; either way, it must have been nice. Maybe there'd been the spray from the waves hitting those sheltering rocks, and the heat of the day must have been deep underfoot in the sand. Pretty, on a clear night with the stars and the moon; even if the fog rolled in, it still would be nice.

Heaven or earth, Cousin? And the guy? Anyway, he was there. And since she was there, it must have been, had to be, nice.

Cousin, thank you for taking me there. I don't think I said anything then. I just walked around that rock and listened while you talked about her, talked and talked as you sat on that sparse grass that grew in the sand.

::

As you said then, she wouldn't have adopted those two kids if she'd expected to die. First the girl, then a few years later the boy. I wonder if she was planning to take another one, or two, or more and more. Right up to when it happened, everyone said wasn't it something how happy she was, and how good she was at raising those kids. Because whatever it is in people that wants to shelter and care for, in her it was something those surgeons could never cut out.

She always looked so good on the outside, and while we all knew, even me, that she wasn't all right inside, we always thought that between her husband and those kids and the doctors, between all those hands outside and inside, she'd find a way to steal another year every year.

It wasn't so common then, Cousin, but with the inside taking the outside like that, cremation made sense. As she'd said once, if her body was going to give her so much trouble, it was the only way to give it some back, to someday get

rid of it for good. And they say that from the time you re-
turned until the burial, and even though her husband was
also around, you kept that urn with her ashes with you; you
wouldn't let it out of your sight.

::

You and her husband had flown back with the two kids
and the urn. And, first thing, you'd decided to go and get
the kids haircuts and one for yourself. In the barbershop,
you lifted the boy up into one of the big green waiting
chairs. You put him all the way back into it, and his feet
hardly came over the seat. The girl climbed into the next
chair, but even though she sat on the edge as she swung her
legs, the leather soles of her blue-and-white oxfords barely
scraped the floor.

You put the urn up on a shelf, next to the bottle of hair
tonic. Now, not everyone knew yet—you'd just got home,
and the obituary wouldn't appear until the next day. The
barber looks at the kids and says to you, "Sister in town?"
And you nodded at the urn and said low, right into his ear
so the kids couldn't hear, "She's in the jar." The guy nearly
fainted! But I know that the joke was not really on him but
was one just for her. And she would have laughed, Cousin
—she loved to laugh. And, young as I'd been, I could make
her laugh—do you like to laugh, Cousin? Me too, I like to
laugh.

Now, the boy, no, there's no way he'd remember anything
of her, just as he'd remember nothing of his first mother.
But the girl—do you think there are things she might recall?
Even one thing, or a little bit of one thing?

And then there's the husband. It's true that it was hard
for us when they first got married, because it meant her
moving away. But we'd liked him because he was special to
her. Cousin, the day long after, when I went to see him, I

think he was looking for something of her in me. And I think I was a disappointment to him. Not because there wasn't anything of her but because there was, and, of course, it could only be some little thing.

Yes, he's remarried and all, and has more family. Still, it must not be easy for him, being the only one around there who really knew her. Because to know something people around you don't know can put you outside of them. And then you can't get back in.

::

It wasn't so bad walking down that logging road this morning. And the minute I got to the dirt road a guy on his way to work gave me a ride into town. He went out of his way and drove me right to your house. And I saw your son there, washing my car. He said to go on inside, that his mother had left me some coffee. Anyone miss me? Anyone come by looking for me? Any mail for me? Any calls?

Cousin, if somebody leaves you out all night in the woods, don't lie face up. Not if you're alone. There are only so many stars you can stand, and even with all of them you don't get enough light. Even with the full moon in July, there's just not enough light. So it's really a time to let gravity take you. Turn yourself over, and gravity makes it feel as if the earth presses back.

Cousin, I see you, and, rough or not, you are a diamond. I see you and see through you. And just as with the bark that fell into my hands last night, it's not that I want to remove. I want to receive. But do I ever get the urge to put my hands into something—like dough, or like clay? I never do, do I? And do you ever?

It was last night when I thought about it, Cousin, and now there's something I want to know. A hundred miles inland, where you didn't take me, where the stone with her full name and full years are, and where you finally had to let it go, what's buried there? What's in the jar? A fifty-fifty mix? Sand and ashes? Or is she, all of her, outside and inside, at the base of that rock near the beach? Where we went with one of the trucks. Where I saw you—I saw you!—dig your hands deep into warm sand.

YELLOW DINING ROOM

My girlfriend is trying to say that she doesn't care if he's my best friend from work: before she leaves the room, when he's looking the other way, she holds up her index fingers, which means she wants him out of here by eleven.

Denny is saying, "Maybe I should have looked at the serving lady when the hostess, Mrs. Logan, spoke, or at Mr. Logan when their guest spoke. But when someone's speaking to you, you look at *that* person, right? Not at somebody else in the room. Or maybe I would have got it right about Gordon and Polly if I'd looked just a little bit over everybody's heads, at those yellow walls. Or at anything—if only I hadn't kept looking at the person speaking. After a while, when it got darker in there, they wouldn't have noticed even if I was looking out a window into the garden. But"— Denny says this to me as if he's not sure— "other people must not have to do stuff like that. They must be able to *look* at the person they're listening to and *think* at the same time."

It's hard to know about Denny. He takes a drive up the Hudson to someone's house, and just has to understand why the walls of one room are different from the others. Now, six months after dinner there, he's caught up in thinking about something that happened, and why he got it wrong. But at work he can be very confident and dry. At an auction of science volumes he did last week, he told the bidders that Goethe's book on color theory, though breathtaking to look at, wasn't scientifically sound. Then he paused a second to add that, of course, Goethe, like the encyclopedist Diderot, was a novelist on the side. And, just when I was sure he was going to start the bidding, he added that even way back in the early nineteenth century Goethe found cause to complain that there was just too much printed matter to keep up with. But then the other day, when I showed him a signed copy of *The Meaning of Relativity*, Denny's eyes became serious and sad, and he said, "Einstein was the *kindest* man." Like the guy had been a personal friend of his, and he missed him.

Denny probably got a little unnerved when the first thing Mrs. Logan asked him at dinner was "Ever been married, Mr. Dennis?" Denny tells me about that and then says, "O.k., maybe it's just a casual question." But I know he takes it as if someone's asking if he'd ever been loved. Or been happy. Or had a home. "I mean," says Denny, "she didn't ask me, 'Are you married?' I mean, that I'm not—and, o.k., that I've never been—does it just *show?*"

I tell Denny not to worry about it, that he's had some bad breaks, that forty's not too late to think of starting. He says, "Then she asked me, 'Ever thought of setting up a firm of your own?' What if I'd said that I wasn't brave enough? After all, it does take a certain amount of courage to buy with one's own money. Courage to buy and courage to sell—I mean, maybe the real courage is in the keeping, before you sell. But no, I just rattled on about how I preferred the camaraderie of the workplace. The generous benefits. The profit-sharing plan.

"Not brave enough—I *did* say it," says Denny, "but to the first question. I meant I'd never been in a situation where it didn't require a lot of courage to get married. And then, after I said that, I looked at the two empty chairs across from me, and, as if it were part of my answer, I asked if they thought we ought to call Gordon and Polly; there was, after all—and I remember pausing there, as if I might be being forward—a phone in their guesthouse. Perhaps they'd got the hour wrong.

"If there was any response to that, it went by me," says Denny. "Because Mrs. Logan just says, 'A fine young man such as yourself. Edith here...,' and she looks over at her friend Edith at the far end of the table, 'Edith took a course in marriage once, didn't you, Edith? Why don't you tell Mr. Dennis about it?'

"Then Edith—I don't remember her last name; it'll come to me—Edith says, like a schoolgirl who'd been waiting her turn to speak, 'I'd been standing at a bus stop in the city, and I picked up one of those brochures with the night-course offerings. And, leafing through it, I noted a class called How to Marry a Millionaire. It was to be held not too many blocks east of where I live, and just for one evening. Now, Mr. Dennis, it's a bit droll that I would have an interest in such a course, as I'd been married for most of my seventy-odd years to a millionaire, and been the daughter of one before that. But I just wanted to go—' and here Mrs. Logan interrupts her. 'To observe,' says Mrs. Logan, finishing the sentence for her, probably so Edith wouldn't lower everything by just saying 'out of curiosity.' 'It was a class for women only,' Edith says, 'but there were women of every age and appearance there, I might add. By the way, Mr. Dennis, the instructress said that every fourth term she also offered the course to *men.*'

"Then Mrs. Logan prods her on: 'And what did you take away from the class, Edith?' Edith gathers herself up in her seat and says, 'Well, it all seemed to come down to this: the most important thing about marrying a millionaire is to *marry* him.' Then she stops for a moment, as if waiting for a cue from Mrs. Logan. 'And what else did the instructress say, Edith?' Edith starts out slowly. 'That, if you wanted to carry it to the logical extreme, you should pick a very *old* millionaire. Very old, and *not very well.* Your honeymoon night is none too soon for Emergency Services to arrive.'

"Mrs. Logan looks right at me. 'The logical extreme,' she says. And then she smiles, to put me at ease. 'Not something Gordon and Polly would understand.' She nods at the two empty chairs, as if to tell me that she was not ignoring my question about where they were. 'Both of them so young and so good-looking. And even before marriage they were —how would the instructress put it, Edith?' Edith shifts in her seat to prepare her delivery: 'Million-heir and million-heiress.' 'Right!' puts in Mrs. Logan. Both of them started laughing. 'And neither of us had need of a course, either, did we, Edith?' And then, for the first time, she looks over at Mr. Logan—not, I thought without affection. '*Really,*' says Edith to Mrs. Logan, 'at the time it would have been so much trouble to marry down.' 'Not so much today, but still *some,*' says Mrs. Logan."

Denny takes a deep breath. "The serving lady had come in to remove the dinner plates. If she or the cook, who was holding the door for her, had found anything to be shocked or put off by in any of the conversation, I couldn't tell. What Mrs. Logan and Edith were saying," Denny says to me, "I wouldn't have said in front of them, would you have?'

"I'm sure they're used to it," I say.

"Well, in the dining room, anyway, I hardly looked at the servants," says Denny. "But I do remember looking at my watch. Eight-forty-five. Dinner had been planned for seven. Mr. and Mrs. Logan and their friend Edith and I had waited in the living room until seven-thirty before we'd come in to sit down. Perhaps Gordon and Polly hadn't heard the time right, I thought. Unlike me, they'd been to Mr. and Mrs. Logan's before—maybe dinner was customarily at eight. And maybe Mr. and Mrs. Logan usually didn't seat everybody until a half hour after that. But now the salad course was being served. And then I was wondering out loud if we should turn on some lights. Again, if there was any response to my question I didn't notice. 'Such a fine summer evening,' says Mrs. Logan, looking nowhere in particular. 'I think you two,' meaning Mr. Logan and me, 'have been very wise in deciding to leave looking at those dusty books till morning.' "

::

People often do as much damage bringing books in to us as has been done in five hundred years. The company knows what they're doing when they send us out to get them. Denny's always available to make the overnight trips to the clients, and I do the estates—up and back on Saturdays, a little country trip with my girlfriend. The first thing I noticed about most of these estates was that although a lot of the furniture was missing, and paintings had obviously been taken from the walls, the bookshelves were always full, never any empty spaces. Some great missed opportunities for the survivors. And some of those books have been there for generations—unread, the pages uncut.

"I think if I did start on my own," says Denny, "I'd specialize. Children's books—you know, they don't have to be so old. Anything from the first half of this century, if it's in good condition.

"If I left, you think the boss would wish me the best? I wish almost everyone the best. But you've got to keep watching what people do. If there's not much doing, then you have to try and go by what they say.

"The first thing Polly said to me was 'How *interesting!*' That was when Mr. Logan, whose book collection I'd come up to inspect, brought me in and introduced me to her and Gordon and left me with them for a bit. I'd just come back to the main house after unpacking my things. 'How interesting,' she said when she found out why I was there. Of course, you hear that a lot, especially from people of means, who are *very* interested in what someone might do out of necessity. Still, I think Polly's interest was sincere. I remember her standing behind the velvet armchair across from me, where her husband was seated, and as she leaned forward, cheek beside his, even he mostly stopped looking at his newspaper and seemed interested.

"Polly told me Gordon's father was an old friend of Mr. Logan's. She said she and Gordon often visited during the summer months, and stayed in one of the guesthouses on the hill above the main house. She asked me which one I was staying in. First one on the path, I told her. 'The pink one? It's lovely,' she said. 'We stayed there once. Now we always use the farthest one, over the crest. Will you be here long? I'd love to learn about old books. Gordon and I have some that were his father's.'

"*People want to know,* isn't that right?" says Denny to me, as if I'd understand exactly what he meant. "Don't tell the boss," he says, "but if I meet people I feel familiar with, I tell them to forget about the things I have to look for in books. I take them aside and recommend a good reprint. I was just about to say that to Gordon and Polly when Mr. Logan came back and said he wanted to show me around the grounds. 'We're having dinner at seven,' he told them. Polly leaned down closer to Gordon, who lowered his paper. They said to us, almost in unison, 'See you at dinner!' "

::

So in about ten minutes my girlfriend is going to come out and do a little walk around the room with her index fingers flashing up and down to remind me that she and time really exist. I think you have to be flexible with friends sometimes, but she says, How often do we go over to *his* place? Still, I think Denny is, in his own way, considerate. Right now, he's laying out magazines all over the coffee table to protect it when he puts his feet up. In the long view of things, why shouldn't he get comfortable? All of a sudden he looks around the living room and glances past all the doors.

"Yeah," say Denny. "All white. White, or off-white, yeah. And that's the way it was at the Logans'. She gave me a tour of the house, and I saw only all-white or off-white rooms, except for one. You know, I don't think I could even tell you exactly where the place was. Somewhere near the Putnam-Westchester county line. I took my time driving there; I got on the Palisades Parkway so I could drive up the west side of the Hudson and through Harriman State Park, where I crossed back to this side. Somewhere near there.

"O.k.," he goes on. "I *did* finally see them at dinner. After a while, I couldn't even *imagine* that anybody was going to sit in those two empty chairs. I looked past them, and that's when I first began to notice what Mr. and Mrs. Logan had done—something I thought was strange. The area where they ate breakfast and lunch, which was just off the kitchen and faced south and east, they'd painted, like the rest of the house, some shade of white. But the dining room, which faced south and west and caught the long, slow sunsets that are warm and yellow anyway, they'd painted yellow. But then I thought, Well, *now* the sunlight's there, because it's summer. For most of the year, though, they'd be eating dinner by artificial light. So the yellow walls would add warmth then. But by the time I'd thought of that, it was so late you couldn't tell what color the walls were anyway.

"That's when I heard Polly's voice through the screen door. 'Should we light some candles?' she said. 'Here, I'll do it,' said Gordon, as they came in, and I saw him let go of her hand to reach into his pocket for matches. The second they sat down beside each other, they made a nearly simultaneous move to hold hands again. I noticed a slight sheen on his brow, and his hair wasn't as tidy as before. Hers was all tousled, and her face was flushed—less like porcelain than I'd remembered it from that afternoon.

"The serving lady brought in some plates of food for them, as if their being late were a regular occurrence. In the next hour or so, Gordon and Polly often held hands, but never looked into each other's eyes or spoke to each other, as if to do so would be to flaunt something. After dinner, again hand in hand, they walked me out through the garden and the tangle of trees, then along the path that led to the guesthouses. At mine, they'd said, 'See you at breakfast!'— again almost in unison. Then they turned to walk up over the hill. But," says Denny, "I didn't see them at breakfast.

"Nice life—I remember thinking that as I tried to get to sleep that night. And I didn't mean the money. I had sat there all evening worrying about Gordon and Polly missing dinner, because I forgot—maybe I don't even know—that two people can find such pleasure in each other that they forget about time. I didn't sleep well that night and was kidding myself if I thought it was just the strange bed. Because I don't think I've really slept very well since—and it's been six months. Do you believe something like that could have such a long-lasting effect?" Denny looks at me, but I don't think he wants an answer.

"So I had breakfast with Mr. and Mrs. Logan and Edith the next day, chose among the books, got the contracts signed, and left just before noon. Gordon and Polly didn't appear, but by then I was making allowances for them. I drove back on this side of the Hudson. I remember stopping to pick up a few groceries—at the unhistoric Stop & Shop in historic Dobbs Ferry—and still I got back to the city by two. Anyway, I didn't see any of those people again until today.

" 'I know you, don't I?' I hear a woman's voice saying. I

was on my way to the Surrey, on Seventy-sixth, to pick up a book from a client. 'I know you,' I hear, and then I see her, framed by a shop entrance on Madison, but I don't place her right away. I'd only seen her with Gordon.

" 'Now I remember,' she said. 'You came to Mr. and Mrs. Logan's?' 'Of course,' I said. 'Polly. And Gordon, how's Gordon?' 'No more Gordon...,' said Polly, with, I thought, a serious look. I started to say, 'He's not...,' and caught myself. 'Not...,' said Polly, finishing my sentence, 'married to me anymore. Is that what you're trying to say? He's not married to me, and I'm not married to him. We're not married anymore.' But I just kept looking at her as if I didn't understand. 'We're divorced,' Polly said. '*Divorce*—ever hear of it?' And then she asked for my card in case she ever came across any books I might be interested in.

"Well," Denny says to me, "now I have to revise my memory of the whole evening, and maybe everything since. But that doesn't mean I'll sleep any better tonight."

::

Girlfriend aside, I want to go to bed. And it's not that I'm tired of Denny—I'm just tired. I decide to try wrapping it up on a light note. "Denny," I say to him, "so you're not a specialist in everything. But you *know* Polly has at least a million dollars. And now she's *not* married. And she's got your card...."

But then I see Denny's not laughing or even listening to me. He's just sitting there with his feet up on the coffee table, and I guess correctly that he's still running a six-month-old movie of that evening back and forth in his mind, trying to figure out if there was something he hadn't paid enough attention to. "It *was* getting dark," he says after a while, "in that yellow dining room."

JELLY DOUGHNUTS

It's almost 1990, and so far, Simmi hasn't asked me one single question about Buck—not a direct one, not an indirect one, not one. She also doesn't seem a bit interested in hearing anything about when he and I were together, or how we got together, or about us splitting up.

It's probably all right that she doesn't feel any need to know that kind of stuff, because I don't think it would matter much to their being together. But when Buck called just now, I started thinking of the time I'd tried to find out why he was so quiet, and he mentioned his mother, how she'd had a way of speaking *for* him.

"You mean if somebody asked you a question, she'd answer it?"

"No," he said. "It wasn't like that."

"You mean she used to tell you just what to say whenever you had to speak to anyone about something important?"

"No, that wasn't it, either," he said. "When it came to her and me, she had a way of saying things... so that even though she was speaking to me... it was as if I were doing the talking. To her."

::

When Buck came by here this evening, he asked me if I

remembered the lullaby he told me about once. The one his mother would sing to him in Penobscot, then in English.

> *I can just about see them going away.*
> *There she was left*
> *on a little islet.*
> *She began to pick*
> *gooseberries.*

He told me that when he sang it to Simmi, she said, "It's beautiful. But please don't sing it again."

Buck's so interested in finding out what other childhoods might have been like that he's always trying things like that. They usually work. With me, and, I'm sure, others, they've worked. So he already knows, since I'm Simmi's sister, and I knew Buck first, that our mother sang to us:

> *Sleep, baby, sleep.*
> *The large stars are the sheep....*

She sang it in four languages—Polish, Yiddish, German, and English. Mama would still sing it to Simmi anytime, if Simmi would just call her and ask her to.

Yes, Buck's heard it from me, but he hoped to hear it from Simmi, who's on to his wanting to know what it was like for her, growing up in Larchmont.

::

Last month, on her first day in New York with me, I arranged for my little sister to go to my stylist and get the works. Simmi didn't know it, but I made the appointment while she was already on her way there. Not everybody in the place was clued in to what was going on; I heard that when the woman who does my facials—and is pretty sure she knows everything about me—asked Simmi how she heard about her, and Simmi said, "I'm Etta December's sister," the woman kept on applying the steam mist and said, "Etta doesn't have a sister."

When Simmi told me that, I started to tell her about something a woman who lived with Buck in 1987 said to me, but the second I said "1987," Simmi broke in to say that it seemed like an awfully long time ago, so I just let the story trail off.

I guess I was wondering if she'd be interested to know that Buck can play guitar. I only found out by chance, when Buck and I were in Prospect Park one day and he noticed a boy with an electric guitar and a little battery-powered amp who was having some trouble tuning up. Buck says to him, "Here, let me try." He tuned it, started playing, people gathered round; it was a scene. And it was like Buck was somebody else. After a while he gave the guitar back to the boy, and we kept on walking. I said, "Buck, you could earn a living at that." He just laughed. Then he told me how he'd taught himself to play guitar when he was little. He and his mother saved up to buy one, and she arranged for him to keep it with some people who lived at the other end of town and to practice in their garage. Buck didn't say anything else, as if that had been a normal way of doing things, so after a while I say, "Why?"

"Why what?"

"Why did you have to keep and play the guitar at someone else's house?"

"Oh," he said; then, "Dad." A few steps later, he said, "So there were only a couple of times I ever got to play for Mum."

If I don't know much about Buck, others probably know less. The woman I'd started to mention to Simmi, the one he'd lived with for most of '87, I'd seen at a Christmas party he took her to back then. She and I were just sitting around, there was no problem, and then, to make small talk, I said, "Isn't it something when Buck picks up a guitar?"

She got almost hostile; I could see she thought I was playing some trick on her, and she says, probably the same way the woman doing Simmi's facial did, so sure, so coolly, "Buck can't play guitar."

::

Last week Buck told me, there he is walking up Broadway with his arm around Simmi, and he doesn't say anything to her, but when he sees something in a store window that he thinks she might like, and lets go of her a moment while he goes to look closer—the instant his arm's not there, Simmi won't take another step in any direction. She's saying, "What happened to *me?* What happened to *me?*" Buck says that if I walked by and I wasn't her sister, I'd think Simmi was kidding. Because then she says, "Just a minute ago—no, just a *second* ago—I was here. What happened to *me?*" She's a riot; she's so funny, anyone would think. If she is being funny, it's just at the very first, the same as when someone smiles without really meaning to.

So Buck tells her he was just looking at something he thought she'd like. "Something for you, Simmi."

She says, "Who, me? Who's *me?* There was a me who was walking with someone, but then the *someone* wasn't there. So what happened to *me?*"

Buck told me that he knew he couldn't win this one. Simmi wouldn't walk toward him or away, and of course she wouldn't swear or anything like that. So rather than have her get upset, he has to take the, oh, five steps to put his arm around her and steer her to the window. But of course by then whatever had caught his eye was beside the point, so they turned away together and kept on walking.

::

Simmi's only been in New York three weeks, but the sec-
ond night she was here Buck took her to a coffee place he
knew, and now Simmi makes sure he takes her there every
night. Maybe if there's somewhere else they have to be,
something one of them *has* to do, they'll skip a night, but
they couldn't miss too many, because then it would become
something they used to do. And that would make it part of
the past. And what she thinks is part of the past Simmi
won't consider.

I've been telling Buck, "She trusts you. If she didn't, she
wouldn't do any of that stuff. She'd just walk away, get out
the credit cards Papa gave her, and start in on that endless
driving again."

I want to help Buck, because I really started all this. I
asked Simmi to come to New York for a visit and then orga-
nized that instant party with my automatic dialer. I'd known
it wasn't going to be easy to get Simmi to come to New
York at all, and that it would be even harder to get her to
stay. The only thing the idea had going for it was that Simmi
hadn't ever spent much time in New York, so there was a
chance she wouldn't think of it as part of the past. I could
tell she might even be looking forward to coming when she
called to ask if I'd send her the Manhattan yellow pages,
care of general delivery somewhere in Arizona, where she'd
be in a couple of weeks. After that I got a fax from Col-
orado, giving the name of someplace in New Mexico where
I could send her the white pages. I knew that Simmi was try-
ing to get a head start on figuring the city out. That's good, I
thought; she's acting as if she's never been here before.

But if she had a theory for it, it didn't quite work out.
She got here at four in the morning. Took a nap. Took a
bath. Took a walk. And then she was ready to leave. So I

told her I was having a party that evening—that I'd forgot to tell her—and that I was treating her to the works at my stylist in the afternoon. She said o.k., she'd get her hair cut or something, and she could leave after the party, when there wouldn't be much traffic; so I said that people don't even *start* arriving at my parties until really late. Then, while she was at the stylist, I phoned everybody on my automatic dialer.

"You know," I said to Buck, "if she hadn't taken to trusting you at that party, she'd have been tail-lights over the Triborough the very next day."

::

My name is, or was, Etta Dietz, and I was lucky to be born in New York City in 1952. My sister Simmi was born, also lucky to be born, in 1954, but just before she arrived my parents moved about twenty miles out of the city, to Larchmont, where Simmi was delivered.

Buck, born *something* MacIsaac on March 26, 1955, was my boyfriend for, at most, four weeks in 1985. Now, in 1990, he has been the boyfriend of my sister, Simmi, for three weeks and holding. Buck was born in Bangor, Maine, at the hospital closest to where his parents lived, in a one-story bungalow on a long triangular lot, on the road between Orono and Old Town.

I hadn't really seen much of Buck in the past five years. Maybe on the street, and maybe once in a while at a party somewhere. I hardly ever saw him, but I did put his number on my automatic dialer in 1985, and I never took him off. Now, because of that, I've seen him a lot in the last three weeks, because he either stops here to pick up Simmi on his way home from work or, even if he knows she's not here, drops by anyway to ask me a question about something that Simmi's done or hasn't done, said or won't say.

Buck isn't known for being very talkative. Otherwise, on the phone just now I would have asked him, "Buck, were you lucky to be born?" Of course, I wouldn't have meant it in the same sense that Simmi and I were lucky, which is *at all*, or in the very best sense, which is *and every minute since*, but just how it looks now to him.

It may be that Buck is not always good at explaining things, but I think he's a good listener. Over the years, I told every one of my boyfriends the most important story of all my family's stories, and as far as I know, and this was even before he knew Simmi, he's the only one who gave up eating jelly doughnuts on the spot and forever.

::

"I was eleven and Simmi was nine," I'd told Buck, "and it was in our house in Larchmont. My father goes out and buys a big bag of fresh jelly doughnuts.

"It wasn't that we'd never eaten jelly doughnuts before, but he and my mother had decided that the day had come that we were both old enough to understand what they went through living in Poland during the war. How they survived to get out after, to America.

"Papa said that as the Germans advanced he and Mama fled from the town where they lived, near the southern border—to Warsaw, but not to the ghetto. Papa wasn't Jewish, but he had to hide Mama, who was. He hated to walk in the street for fear that someone who knew who he was married to might inform on him, or that the authorities might follow him back to her.

"Before, my parents both had good professions, but now they were in hiding, in some small rooming house. They had to make a living quietly, and somehow they settled on jelly doughnuts. There were lots of cafés, and many of their suppliers were disappearing.

"Papa used the bit of money they had to buy flour, eggs, shortening, sugar, and jam. But he was afraid to hire just anybody to deliver the doughnuts. Then he noticed a little boy who'd lost his parents. 'He was even younger than you are now,' Papa said to Simmi. 'And he probably didn't really know that he was Jewish. And, like your mama and your sister here, he had blue eyes and was fair—that was good, because he could blend in with the general population.' And they took him in, like a son, and as a delivery boy.

"They taught him where to deliver the doughnuts and how to collect the money. They told the boy to take only gold coins, because the Polish money was worthless. At the time, jelly doughnuts were a boon to the cafés, but Papa said that didn't mean he and Mama were living well or anything—they spent just enough to feed themselves, pay expenses, and but more supplies to make the doughnuts. Because if they wanted to be able to save for their escape, the had to live very simply.

"Papa said everything went o.k. for about nine months, and then one day a Gestapo man followed the little boy home. If it had been a younger agent—they were more ideological—it would have been the end. But it was an older man, and he was on the take. He demanded a cut. So he began to collect a percentage from them, and that made it more difficult to save money. They worked even harder, for about three more months, and then one day the boy didn't come back on time. They waited and waited. Then somebody from one of the cafés sent word that the boy had been taken away. So Mama and Papa took the gold coins they'd saved and sewed them under the buttons of their coats, inside the lining, and fled eastward that night.

"Papa said to us, 'And in all that time, girls, because those doughnuts were all that we'd had to sell in that whole year we never ate one of them.' Mama added that whenever Papa had sprinkled the powdered sugar over the finished ones his Adam's apple would go up and down with desire.

"Then Papa opens the bag, takes out the jelly doughnuts he'd just bought, and puts them on little plates and passes them around. 'One for Simmi. One for Etta. One for Mama. And one for me.' We all started to eat—all except Simmi. That's the first time I ever saw that expression she still gets. We looked at her and her eyes were wet, and wide with fear, and she said, 'What about the *boy?* Where did they take the *boy?*' "

::

If Buck drops by my place when Simmi's not here, he's not coming to complain—he's just trying to understand. "Simmi won't even let me talk about what we had for lunch the day before," he might say. Or "What happened to Simmi?" he'll ask. What in the past, he means. I always tell him to believe me, nothing ever did. "But now you are," I say to Buck. "Now you are, and you're the only thing that's ever really happened to Simmi."

The evening Buck stopped in to ask me if I'd noticed that Simmi never swears, I had to tell him why—it was part of the past, so Simmi never would. I told him that when she was little she heard one of mother's friends use the word "ass." It wasn't a word Mama ever used, so later Simmi asked her if what the lady said was a bad word. And Mama didn't want Simmi to think her friends were saying bad words so she said, "It's really not." But then the next time the lady came over and said to Simmi, "How are you doing today?" Simmi gave her a big smile and said, "I fell on my ass." Simmi got sent to her room, and everyone was all flustered. That was the last time anybody heard her swear.

::

Buck's never actually come out with it, but sometimes I think he wants to know why Simmi and I are so unalike. The closest thing I can come to explaining it to myself is that it's as if the same light has fallen on different films.

When I turned thirteen and moved up to another school, I changed my last name. It all went more or less according to plan, and I think all plans probably involve some fear. But the more I watched the war documentaries on television, and the more I read about Poland during the Second World War, and the more I asked Papa questions, the more I figured that if my Jewish mother could make jelly doughnuts there, in the middle of Warsaw, and survive inside the shifting borders of Poland from 1938 to 1945, I could be brave enough to change my name from the German spelling, "Dietz," which Papa'd changed it to for protection, back to "Dec," the Polish spelling. So I wrote "Etta Dec" on every school form in grade 7, and after a few days my homeroom teacher came down on me and said, "Etta, what sort of name is Dec?" I didn't want to explain, and that's when I started telling people, "It's short for 'December.' "

::

I might have thought about it later—what happened to the boy—but Simmi noticed right away. I remember we all stopped eating and Papa told us he had heard that the boy was sent to a concentration camp, but that he must have got away. Someone who knew that Papa and Mama had survived and gone to America saw and talked to the boy, who was working on a ferryboat between Italy and Malta. And that person wrote to somebody in Poland, who wrote to somebody in America who told them.

"So," Papa says to Simmi, "the boy was all right. Now you can eat your jelly doughnut."

But Simmi just looks at the doughnut on her plate and

asks, "Did he—did the boy ever eat one of the jelly doughnuts you and Mama made?"

"No, none of us did."

"Then," said Simmi, "I think I'd rather have ice cream." So the rest of us didn't finish our doughnuts and we all ate ice cream instead.

I've been thinking about this a lot lately. When Buck heard the story from me—even though he didn't know or ask anything about Simmi, and even though he and I weren't together for very long after that—right then, on the spot and forever, he stopped eating jelly doughnuts.

::

"*Safe* with me? *Comfortable* with me?" That's what Buck said, the day after the party, when I told him how I thought Simmi felt with him. "And of all the guys on my automatic dialer I'm glad it was you," I told Buck. "And she even got to sleep with you."

Buck said, "I really wouldn't call it—well, it was sleeping *only*. She wouldn't even let me take my leather jacket off; when I started to, she gave this little shake of her head to say no." Buck looked at me as if he didn't know what was going on. "Safe with me? Comfortable with...?" She had him so afraid of seeming forward that he kept his boots on. "*Breathing* together, maybe. And sometimes our kneecaps touched under that old opened-up cotton sleeping bag— that was it."

Simmi hadn't wanted to use my convertible sofa, so they'd slept beside it on a small rug, with Buck facing her, she in her wool sweater and jeans, nestled where the floor met the wall.

::

"Puh. Puhnub." My father just couldn't get it right when he heard it the first time. Almost like when he first heard "crunchy granola" and thought it was one long new word.

"Puh-nob-scot" I said it slow into the phone. "Penobscot. Well he's half Penobscot, really."

Almost twenty years in the city, and I've never met a man that I've trusted like Simmi trusts Buck. I mean *I* even met Buck, but it wasn't so much that I trusted him—for me, I think, it was those high cheekbones and that straight, jet-black hair. But Simmi had only been in New York about twenty hours before she did—Simmi, who gets uncomfortable if a man even looks at her.

When I called my parents in Coral Gables, where they live now, and told Papa about it, and that I didn't think Buck could support her, right away he said, "I'll send checks." He said that anything was better than that constant motel-to-motel movement of hers. That he wouldn't go broke either way. "If only we can get her to just stay in one place," he said.

After I got out of college, I had a way of advancing from job to job, but when Simmi graduated she would start out on one thing, then quit for an entirely other kind of thing. It didn't seem to matter so much at the time, because, even though she was changing jobs, she was always working. Now it matters, because she doesn't want to do any job she's done before, so there's almost nothing that she'll do.

I've been telling Buck and everybody not to get Simmi wrong. She likes to work. It's just that you can tell by the look of fear in her eyes when someone says to her, "Why don't you work in public relations?" and she says, "No, I worked in public relations," that it's useless saying to her, "Yes, but this is a different city, you'd be at a different firm, and you could try a different position there."

When I told Buck about calling Papa, he said he felt a little funny about the money part, but he'd agree as long as we let Simmi know all about it, so we did. Then Buck says to Simmi and me that our parents sounded really interesting, and it would be nice if they came up for a visit. So Simmi wouldn't have to say anything, I said to Buck, "They kind of like the idea of Simmi better than the real Simmi." When Buck asked just what that meant, Simmi came right out and said, "It means they love me better when I'm not around them."

Of course, I hadn't told Buck or Simmi the whole story. During the call, Papa said that if Buck every wanted to marry Simmi, he'd buy them an apartment. And when Mama got on the phone she said that if they did get married then maybe Simmi would think, There, that's that, and then she'd get on with whatever she was supposed to do in life. But I told them that I thought the best thing to do at this point was just to take it one check at a time.

Mama and Papa both made me promise to try to get Buck to talk to Simmi about getting professional help. I hate it when they bring it up, because I never know if they're right or wrong. But I said that sooner or later I would. Then, before we finished the call, Papa said I should make sure to tell Buck about the jelly doughnuts too, so he wouldn't bring some home by mistake and ruin everything, and I said to him, "Don't worry, Papa, he already knows," which was the truth.

::

If you ask Buck if that's his real first name, he'll just answer, "My mother always called me Buck." I think it's his way of making sure everyone calls him Buck now, here in New York.

He's never told me much about his growing up in Maine, just a little bit now and then, to get me talking. He would always look at me with wonder whenever I'd tell him stories of my girlhood, about how Mama would put us on the train, and Papa would meet us in the city, and take us somewhere for ice cream, and then say, "Now to the stinky children's zoo!"

If you asked Buck what he might have been doing on a summer afternoon in 1963, he'd just say something like "Oh, making stuff. In the back yard." He wouldn't tell you that he was using scrap lumber he'd gathered to build birdhouses to sell by the side of the road, and that that's how he helped pay for his guitar, and that he really liked to work with wood, so he got good at it, and that's how he became a cabinetmaker.

To find just that much out, I had to ask him about a dozen questions. Because Buck can't believe that anybody could find those things interesting.

I've always thought Buck has too many preconceptions of what a normal childhood's like. Even if there were some things he missed, he shouldn't confuse them with what might make him happy now. He has this idea that there's some certain way to be, that it's all around and he's not in on it, but when he asked me something about Simmi the other day I told him, "You think you want to be with somebody cheerful, and have everything in place. If that happens and you're happy, fine. But what if that happens and you're not?"

Buck has admitted to me that there are times when he starts to think that Simmi's trying to tell him he really isn't so different from her. One day he took her along to Connecticut to look at some cabinet restoration work outside Stamford, and when they got near the exit to Larchmont, he said, "We could stop off."

"Sure," she said, "Someday when we're on our way back from Bangor." Bangor, Orono, Old Town—you can tell that those places seem very far away to him, and Larchmont so near, but of course he hadn't been thinking how it all might have seemed to Simmi.

::

When Buck came by earlier this evening, he told me that he and Simmi were out for a Sunday-afternoon walk yesterday, and that they bumped into a couple of designers he was building cabinets for. Buck stopped to talk to them, but a pizza delivery must have gone by, because all of a sudden Simmi started sniffing the air and tugging at his arm, saying, "Buck, I smell pizza. Let's get out of here."

Things like that about Simmi aren't news to me. I could have just explained to Buck that, first, it has nothing to do with pizza, because you can take her to a pizza place where you can see pizza and smell pizza and eat pizza at the same time, and everything's o.k. But to just *smell* it without at least *seeing* it—that might make her start thinking of someplace she went for pizza in, say, 1988. Or even 1968. I could have told him that, but I thought this was a good time to keep my promise to my parents instead.

"You know, Buck," I said. "There are people who think maybe Simmi needs to see, you know, some kind of shrink. But of course I tell them that then they'd better take up a collection to send you through shrink school. Still, maybe if we could find a good professional... and you could talk to Simmi... maybe go with her...."

But Buck just ran both his hands at once over those high cheekbones of his and through that shining jet-black hair. It seemed to leave his eyes extra clear as he fixed them right on mine and said, more firmly than I'd ever heard him speak, "She was right about the doughnuts."

I just nodded. Yes, she was right about the doughnuts, quick about the boy.

::

So this evening he left here about a quarter after five, and I was surprised when he called me about an hour ago, at eleven-thirty, while Simmi was taking a bath. He said something about how he'd tried to make an issue out of the things that were bothering him, to see what he could get Simmi to say. And he especially wanted to get her to swear. He said they had dinner, and then she was lying on his sofa, reading a book, and he was on the floor, using her leg to prop his elbow on while he read the paper. When she says isn't it time for them to start heading out for coffee, though he's got nothing against it, he starts in on her that maybe they shouldn't go there so often, or maybe only on alternate nights, or one week to one coffee place and another week to another. He's trying to get her angry, but after he keeps it up for a bit her eyes go full of fear—first wide, then wet. "And then," Buck says, "I swore *for* her. And after a while we did go where we always go for coffee, thought by that time it didn't seem like such a big deal."

Yes, they went, but not right away. Because Simmi said, "I think I'll read my book some more before we go." Buck thought she was even smiling a little when she said it. That was after he said, "Turn around. Turn around so I can kiss you."

CARMEN

It doesn't happen on the Wednesdays, when Carmen's meeting her mother at LaGuardia. Every time, for the past few years, it's when her mother's about to leave, during those final steps to the airport bus. Last trip it was math. "Carmen, honey. It's thirteen years since that stuff with Eddie."

"Ma—"

"Eighteen and thirteen is thirty-one, honey. What about the next...."

And the trip before that: "Carmen, if you could keep your eyes on one guy—"

"Ma, there's nothing wrong with my eyes; it's these *guys!*"

It's almost too much for Carmen to think of when she tries to follow it back. Her mother didn't go to college, because of getting married. Then she herself didn't get married—but she didn't go to college, either.

Her mother, when she was the age for it, was all "What's he like? What's he like?" That's the way Carmen's Aunt Jean, her mother's sister, tells it, and how Carmen's parents got together. Aunt Jean had been seeing some guy while she was finishing her last year of high school, but kept putting him off because she was getting ready to go to college. Then he catches the eye of her little sister, just one grade down, who starts asking what he's like.

Aunt Jean said she knew it was going to be trouble because her little sister had also started talking about home not feeling like home anymore and, gee, sometimes she'd sure like to get out of the house. From the very first week Aunt Jean went away, she started sending presents back, one a week—Ohio State sweatshirts, T-shirts, pins—to try to make the idea of college more real, to get her sister to hold out one more year.

That same guy her aunt put off back then her mother took on. And it was the same week in November the pregnancy test came back that the bookmark with the college song, "Carmen Ohio," on it arrived.

" '*Carmen,*' that's a nice name." That's what her Aunt Jean told her her mother said. That if it was a girl that's what she'd call her. "Your mother didn't really have much on her mind in those days, Carmen."

"Aunt Jean! I was named after a bookmark?"

::

As far as Carmen could tell, from all the things she could remember, her parents' marriage had never been good. What could it be like for her mother? Because she always finds in her own life that when it's not working out either she starts to forget or she starts to remember what life's all about.

Her Aunt Jean, a few years after graduating from college, moved out to the state of Washington and got married. She wrote back to her sister that she'd heard things weren't so good for her, to bring Carmen and come out there to live. Carmen had read the letter when her mother left it in the telephone-table drawer. But they didn't go. All Carmen's been able to figure out in all the time since is that her mother didn't ever want to do anything that made it look like she'd made a mistake, even if staying was a bigger one.

::

Maybe other mothers thought the kind of things her mother would say; Carmen didn't know. Once, a woman her mother's age came into their tuxedo-rental place and said, "You sure are lucky, Mrs. Mitchell. You get to be around so many *men*."

Carmen's father wasn't far—he had to have heard. Carmen's mother looked at the woman as if she were focusing, concentrating, compressing before she delivered her response, full but not loud, and through a narrow smile. "Men?" And then, as if it were music, she let a few silent beats go by before finishing. "I *hate* men."

Carmen had a good view, standing there behind the cuff-link showcase, with her mother and the woman in front. She could see for a few seconds the woman didn't know how to take it, but then her mother's smile broadened, which made it look as if she were just joking, which allowed the woman to smile also.

Carmen wasn't even in high school yet, but she already knew her mother always chose her words carefully. Since she's been out on her own and thought about it, she's realized that though there are many things beyond her mother's control, at least her thoughts and her words are her own.

Even in those days, when she was helping her parents after school in the shop, Carmen would look at her mother speak and notice she never seemed to start a sentence until she was sure of the end of it. And even after they enlarged the place, when Carmen couldn't always get a clear view of her mother saying the things she said, Carmen could still imagine, from the tone of her mother's voice, the exact look on her face.

::

At first it *was* all men, because they'd conceded the wedding-dress trade to the women's shop down the street, but when Carmen was in tenth grade her mother prodded her father into taking over the small store next to theirs. They broke through a wall to make a large arch, and in the new part they put the women's section, with wedding dresses, bridesmaids' outfits, flower-girl things.

Her father mostly avoided that area, while her mother roamed in and out of both. Before the shop expanded, if a bride-to-be came along to help her future husband pick out a style for his tux, Carmen's mother might say to her, especially if the bride was very young, "Are you sure you're doing the right thing?" Meanwhile, Carmen's father would be kneeling on the floor, trying to call out measurements to her mother, who was supposed to be putting them down on a form sheet. But her mother would still be turned to the bride. "Have you talked it over with your mother?" Her voice was clear and low. "Do you know what it can mean to be married?"

At times like these, the grooms invariably deferred to Carmen's mother as some kind of wit, and her father, down near the ground level, couldn't say or do much about it. The business may have been his, as it had been his father's before him, but he could never control what his wife thought about it. And, when customers were there, the things she might say. "Wait a while," she'd tell the brides-to-be. "Maybe come back in five years—we'll *still be here.*"

::

The worst thing for Carmen about the stuff with that boy in their town, Eddie, was that she really didn't know what her father thought about it. Not then and not now. If he really did think she should marry the boy and stay around town, shouldn't go to Ohio State—if there was any possibility at all that that's what her father was thinking—she didn't want to know. But not knowing made her even more fright-

ened then than she already was. Just another reason now for
not going back home.

"Carmen...," her mother had said to her when she asked.

"Well? What *does* Daddy think?"

"Carmen, honey..., I know you've got your heart set on
Ohio State—but I just don't think Columbus is far enough
away."

Well, Eddie *had* said to Carmen, "You think I can't drive
over to Columbus and find you?" Yes, she knew he could.
He could find her by phoning her dorm or hanging around
outside, or at the part-time job she had waiting at the
Lazarus department store downtown. He could bother her.
He could make her nervous. And it would be when she was
new in Columbus, new in the dorm, new at work.

"Carmen...," her mother had said softly, standing in the
doorway of Carmen's room, reaching behind herself and
producing one of those little squarish suitcases that you
hardly ever see anymore—train cases, Carmen thought they
were called. Women always used to carry them. Inside they
had five-by-eight-inch mirrors, fitted sideways into the top
part, and elasticized pouches along the edges, with bobby
pins or grit left in them from some previous trip.

This was a dull-blue-green one her mother was holding.
Carmen looked at it, then at her mother. "Ma, am I going
out to Washington to stay with Aunt Jean?"

"You're going to New York. There's a place you might
like there—it's a hotel where I stayed that trip Daddy
couldn't go. I liked it so much I wanted to live there."

Her mother had entered Carmen's room and started
packing, as if it were she, not her daughter, who was going.
"I know it's late, honey, but maybe in the dark is the best
time to leave. I'll drive you to the bus station and wait with
you. I can send you more dresses and things later." Her
mother packed the case better and quicker than Carmen
could have herself. And whichever drawer her mother's

hand went to Carmen didn't mind. She hadn't thought about it before, but there was really nothing anywhere that she was hiding from her mother.

::

As long as it was August, it was fine there in the Gramercy Park Hotel. But as soon as the calendar said September, Carmen had to keep reminding herself why she wasn't in Columbus.

During the three weeks in August, she hadn't really done much besides taking the check that would have been her tuition and dorm fees to a bank around the corner and opening her account. That was probably the biggest thing—there seemed something very final about it.

The rest of the days were more or less the same. In the morning she read every word in the newspaper over a long breakfast. In the afternoon she napped and read magazines. She would always go down for dinner *after* she watched the news on television—it broke up the evening, and when she came back to her room it was almost time to get ready for bed.

Then, for the first two weeks in September, she really wanted to call Ohio State to find out what the textbooks were for the courses she would have taken. So she could sit in her hotel room in New York and read them. Was that so strange? She started thinking that there was nothing about herself she couldn't explain—explain *away*, she thought—in a few seconds. If there had been anyone asking.

From her hotel room, the stuff with Eddie began to become clearer to her. When it happened, it had taken her completely by surprise; she didn't understand what was going on. After all, she didn't know him that well, even if he had graduated from her school the year before. But there he was, all of a sudden, calling her. Just small talk, and then he could say, in different ways, that he wanted to see her in a wedding dress. And she always seemed to be running into him, near her house, or near the shop. Then it got worse. "Your long dark curls and a long white gown—hey, rosy cheeks?"

"Stand a pretty little thing like that around all those wedding dresses and what do you expect?" the policeman who came to take the report had even said to her mother. He said they would, if she wanted, send someone around to talk to the boy and his parents, but that might not produce the desired effect. That a court order of protection could be requested, but it's just a piece of paper. And since the boy really wasn't threatening her—what he was doing was asking her to get married—a judge might not take it too seriously. "Maybe it's harassment, and maybe it isn't," the policeman said. "Either way, she can keep saying no."

::

Those first few weeks in New York it was no good calling her mother every day, collect or not. Whether she called the house or the shop, her father almost always answered, and when she asked to talk to her mother her father would stand by the phone while they talked, so her mother really couldn't say much about how she was doing. And the times she did get her mother alone all Carmen wanted to ask her was "Now what do I do?" But she began to realize that her mother couldn't answer that, so after the first couple of weeks she called less.

Every day, for those six weeks in the hotel, venturing a little further into her new world, she found herself learning new things in, for her, a completely new way: which newspapers not to buy, which restaurants not to eat at, which apartments not to go see, which jobs not to apply for, who not to give her name to. All this while trying not to cause any problems for her mother and not to be anything like her father, while also trying not to make the same mistakes as her mother.

Mornings, alone, not fully awake, she'd look at the yellowing leaves outside in the morning light, figuring out what she wasn't going to do that day—when going to Ohio State would have been the natural order of things. August was too late to apply to any of the universities in New York, but she knew she wasn't going to start midyear, or the following fall, either. The whole idea had been to go to Columbus after twelfth-grade summer vacation. To her, no other place and time for that was ever going to make sense.

::

Her mother visits her twice a year now, spring and fall. She always arrives on a Wednesday evening and Carmen always meets her plane. And she always leaves on a Sunday afternoon, and lets Carmen go with her only as far as across the street from Grand Central, where she catches the airport bus.

"Ma, can't I—"

"Carmen, honey, I'll be all right."

Every trip her mother leaves it until then: Shouldn't she look for an apartment in a better area; shouldn't she try for a job with some future? "And, you know, someday you *could* get married, Carmen."

It's true that she's never had the same boyfriend two trips in a row. Some of these visits of her mother's she doesn't have a boyfriend at all. The last guy lasted six months, which was about right; if her mother saw her with the same guy twice, she might get her hopes too high.

"It's not easy, Ma. It looks easy, but then maybe their friends have to like you, maybe their family has to like you. And if somebody doesn't like you there's nothing you can do to make them like you—they're going to look for things."

Her mother was married at seventeen, so how could she know of such problems? Because it seems to Carmen it's taken every year of her life in New York to learn them.

So Wednesdays her mother gets there, Fridays and Saturdays Carmen follows her around while she shops, but Thursdays she just takes her mother along to work, a costume-design place in a loft in Chelsea. "They're not *real* wedding dresses, right, Ma?" And her mother's got it all sorted out, after so many trips, that some of the boys there prefer boys, and some of the girls prefer girls. There's not really what you'd call job security, not much health insurance, but it's quiet up on that high floor, and there's never anybody who's not speaking to someone else, so it's an easy place to be for whole days.

::

On the Sunday mornings, when she's leaving, Carmen's mother always counts out some twenties. She squirrels them away for these trips, for Carmen. "Save it or spend it—up to you. You're on your own, anyway." Her mother always tells her something like that.

And Carmen saves it to spend it. Once a year, she'll have two parties. When, in the beginning, she thought of having a party, she started to worry. So many invitations to repay—all those people, and she didn't mean numbers. Then she figured out what to do: two parties, on two nights in a row.

To the first night's party she invites people who may not like each other, but she doesn't really care if they do. To the second she invites people she knows will. So on the first night she worries but doesn't really care; on the second she cares but doesn't have to worry.

Of course, she tells everybody that her place just isn't big enough, which it isn't, to have all those people arrive at one time. And if she thinks one half of a couple could be right for the first night and the other for the second, she feels bad about it, but they both have to come the first night. Because she's trying to get the second night the way she wants it. On the first night she'll have freedom of thought at least, but on the second she's got to also have freedom of speech.

It's on the second night she finishes paying the caterers with those twenties from her mother. She pays them half in advance when she books them, half when the second night's party is just as she wants it to be.

"You *see?*" she says to the caterers, always making a sweep with her hand to include all her guests. Besides herself, the caterers are the only ones ever there on both nights. "You *see?*" She says it every time she has these parties, on the second night. "You *see?*" And she always says it in the same way she answers her mother across the street from the airport bus, every trip now.

"Carmen, honey...," her mother will say, starting to tell her one thing while Carmen looks for a way to tell her another: that she has her own place, she pays her own rent, that some of the people she knows really like each other.

SIX QUARTERS

First, I take off my watch. I put it here on your driveway. Maybe you see me put my head down to look at it so much you think I charge by the minute. You start to worry. First thing I say, "Don't worry." Then I answer you about Six Quarters.

It started with the back and forth. Back and forth across the border. Us on the Mexican side, aunt on the Texas side. Back and forth.

My parents had—they had problems. My old aunt comes over from the Texas side and she sees it—that they have problems—and she takes me and the little brother back to her side, this side. For little bits—weeks, months, maybe whole summers, I don't remember. Back and forth.

But the end of the one summer she doesn't take us back down. She puts us in school on this side, where we weren't even citizens. I had some school on the other side, but the little brother started on this side. My aunt said to my parents to give him his first year on the Texas side. Well, that's how she stole us.

He was just five then. I was almost eight. Today he is different from me. My old aunt did the best she could for me, but I had three years on the other side when I was already old enough to know problems—that they were *problems*.

My aunt, she was my father's aunt. She was old, but my uncle was older by twenty, twenty-one years. No kids of their own. When I came, he was seventy-two, but still work-ing—at this, at that, not so much for money, but to keep busy. And I was always watching. When he would be fixing things, I would watch him, maybe hold things for him. I think I was twelve—so then he was seventy-six—and he was fixing the lawn mower in the driveway. And he had the rosebushes behind him—dark pink roses, and there was dew on them.

Now I see your roses, so maybe even if you don't ask me that question, I tell you all this anyway. Yours are more pink. His were more red, but still pink. Maybe that is not dew on your roses. Maybe you have automatic sprinklers to water at night. But I start to remember anyway.

"Watching, watching," he says. "Always you are watching. Someday you have to start doing." So I am thinking, Well, I'm not going to school like I am to grow up to fix lawn mowers. But it was summer, and I liked my old uncle, so might as well learn. And here I am, thirty years later. Same time of year.

Now, you want to fix a car engine? I can. I can fix it. But car engines have so many *problems*. That's a four-stroke en-gine. That's valves. That's timing. That's an oil pump. That's so many things that your lawn mower, it doesn't have. That's problems, but I could fix it. And now they're making four-stroke lawn mower engines, something like my old uncle never saw.

The four-strokes I can fix, but this little two-stroke you have here, I'm at home with. Not really different from my old uncle's mower. So when you phone me and tell me what lawn mower you have, what problems you have with it, I tell you I'll be there in the morning. I tell you to have waiting one gallon of gas and a half cup of oil to mix—for a two-stroke engine, the oil goes right in with the gas. You know that, but I say it just to make sure. Because I don't carry around gas and oil.

So we mix one ounce of oil with one quart of gas. Oil—one ounce; gas—one quart. Or, as my uncle would say, "quarter." Because a quart is a quarter-gallon. And he said that in the British Empire their quarts—their quarters—are bigger. And in one of their gallons there was almost five of our quarts. "Five quarters!" my old uncle would say, and laugh and look at me like I should laugh, too. "Five quarters!"

::

Yes, my old uncle liked roses. Grew them. He had a way of smelling a rose—after he smelled a rose, you are surprised the rose is still there.

Look here: I check the magneto, the coil, the fly-wheel, the spark plug of your lawn mower. See what good care I take? With your lawn mower? What about *my* lawn mower? Well, me, I don't have a lawn mower, but I know me. Say, with my car—as long as it gets me there. With your car—if I fix your car, I make it just *so*. And you see me look down at my watch—is it to remind you you are paying? Yes, you are paying, but that is not why I look at my watch.

Today, these days, I talk. But for years I don't smile, don't wave, don't talk. I live in ten towns in ten years—ten towns! Five on each side of the border. Some of those towns twice. And you know, the closer to the border those towns are, they are rougher.

The little brother, I lost touch with him. I know he's in Chicago, so I think, I'll go to Chicago. I start out that same day, and I end up, no money, in New York—in New York!

Now, agencies—city agencies, state agencies, federal agencies—a lot of trouble in them. And people with trouble coming to them. But one lady in one agency helped me—sent me to one man in another agency who helped me. Clothes, food, room, and they were, for me, looking for work. Because I am a citizen, you know. I show them—my aunt had it fixed up. Then I tell them, "Small engine repair."

::

But it is not so easy to find just what you want. *Anything,* they say at the agency to me, *anything.* I'd have to do for a while. And I said yes, *anything.*

On a Friday they send me out to see about a job in a repair shop out of the city, in a big store. Maybe you know the store. I go on the train. I am early. I look around the town.

I look in store windows. In one window, first I look in, but then I look at myself, like in a mirror. I think how the man at the job might look at me. I think: Before I see him, I'll cut my hair. I don't see a barbershop, I see a beauty parlor. One woman, first one to the window, her chair is empty. She's leaning back on the counter, reading. A magazine. I don't really want to go in—all women in there—but I tap on the window. I show her with my hand that I want to get my hair cut, for her to come to the door. I want to find out how much to get my hair cut. She holds the door open, stands in the door. Fifteen dollars.

"Fifteen dollars," I say back to her. I don't want to say it's too much, or too much for me. "But my hair is *fun,*" I say. I figure she doesn't see too many like me in there. "It's fun to cut."

I see her holding the door open. "In the chair," she says. I sit, and from the back she touches my hair. "Fun," she says, kind of quiet. She walks around, looks at me, lifts up the hair from my forehead. She says it again. "Fun."

Still, then, I don't talk much. I mean, in those days. But if she's cutting my hair, and there's something about me she wants to know, and she's not getting paid, I think I got to tell. Soon she finds out a lot about me that nobody—nobody around there, maybe nobody around anywhere—knows. Something, not much, about the towns. Something, not much, about my old aunt and uncle. And I tell about the little brother. About the job I go see about. About how then I will go to Chicago. I try not to tell her too much, but I tell her a lot. For finding things out, she has a way.

::

In that chair, I start to forget about Chicago. That was my idea—to get some money, to have some money to get to Chicago. You know, I wasn't even sure how to find the little brother when I get there. And then I am in that chair.

I go see the man; I get the job. I go back to the beauty parlor—because she says to come back, let her know what happens. Everyone in there looks at me, but I tell her. She says, "Wonderful, I'll buy you dinner." Now I feel bad, and I say, "Already you lose fifteen dollars on me." So she says she has food. To come to her place. Now all these women in there look at her. She says for me to sit and wait until she's through with her appointments. She brings me a Coca-Cola and a glass and puts a pile of magazines in front of me. I drink the Coca-Cola but I just look out the window. Except when I look at her—not right at her but I look at her in the mirror. And I don't touch the magazines.

::

I have to tell you the truth that when we go to her apartment I get worried. Big apartment. I think: her mother, her father. What will I say to them? Or sister. Or brother. Or boyfriend. Or husband. I look around. Every door I see, I think someone's going to come out of that door. If you know me in Mexico, in Texas—the life there I was living? Soon *husband* is all I am thinking.

The phone rings. "I'm all right," she says. "Don't worry. He's fun." She looks at me while she talks on the phone.

Then we start eating, talking—mostly her talking. After a while, she talks about me—talks about me! To me! About my hands, my eyes, and then she talks about my hair.

I go out from my little room in the morning to an agency. Take a train not far. And by night I sit in a big apartment with a woman and I drink coffee and she says, "I like to watch you drink coffee." Coffee—watch me drink coffee! I say, "How do I drink it? I just drink it." But I like to hear what she says.

So, no problems. It is not long later that we get married. No problems. I go to work—at the job, no problems. At the apartment, no problems. No problems, no problems, and then behind every door is coming a problem. After work is a problem. Weekends is a problem. Behind every door, her mother, her father. Sisters, brothers. Boyfriends from before. The husband before me. Her stories about them, and stories they told her, she is telling me.

She looks at me. She waits. She tells another story. She waits. But when I think, I remember only two stories—one about me and my old uncle, and one my old aunt told me. Only two stories? So I save them.

Everybody in her stories, it was like they were there. There with her but not with me. It is a problem. I have a problem. So we have problems.

::

Today, you see me smile, answer your question. But before, for ten years, I am not this way. And the day I don't go to the job but take the train into New York City, Penn Station, I am not this way.

I walk over to Grand Central Station. I phone my wife at work and tell her I am going to Chicago. Even with problems, she doesn't want me to leave. Can you believe, like that, I leave? Like that? In me, what kind of life?

I get to Chicago and four days it takes me to find the little brother. I have to phone Texas. I have to telegraph Mexico.

Glad to see me? He is surprised. His wife, she is really surprised. But they have in their house a basement, like an apartment. I get a job in Chicago; I pay to stay. Big repair shop, lots of motorcycles—motorcycles are two-stroke. One month, two months, five months.

Six months, one day I wake up and don't feel good. Next day and next day, I don't feel good. So I think, it's the beer —better not go to the bars. I go downtown. I look in store windows. I stand and read magazines. I drink Coca-Cola. And still I don't feel good. I even go to the doctor.

Well, from doctor to doctor you can go. From beer to Coca-Cola you can go. Even to milk you can go. But if you don't feel at home, you don't feel good.

I think back to what I say to my wife to get her to cut my hair, first time. I get an idea about how to remember stories, so I can tell them to my wife. I try to tell the little brother about it. So he can help me remember.

Well, he is different from me; he looks at his wife, his wife looks at him. He says he can't help. OK, I go by myself down in the basement. I stay for days—I sit up in the bed, I look at the door. But the only stories I think of are the two I already remember. Not much to go back with, but, anyway, I go back.

I take the train from Chicago to New York. It is too early to call unless I call her at work. I think, what if one of those women in there answers? Who knows what they say about me to her for six months?

I sit in Grand Central. I don't drink beer, or Coca-Cola, or milk. I don't look at magazines. I wait. I call her at home. It rings and I am thinking, What if someone else answers? But she answers. "Wait right there," she says. "Don't go *any-where.*"

What is that—sixty, ninety-minute drive back? She is not smiling. I don't say anything. In all that time, she says only one thing. "*Chicago*. You in *Chicago*."

::

You know, I have no job when I come back. Next day, we talk about it. With my own tools, I tell her, I don't need a job. My wife, she buys me my own tools. I get cards printed up. I put them in stores, supermarkets, like where you saw it. Now I will answer your question.

I say to the printer, put in one corner "Lawn Mowers," in one corner "Outboard Marine," in one corner "Motorcycles," in one corner "All Two-Stroke Work," and in the middle in big letters SMALL ENGINE REPAIR. And the phone. The printer says to me, "What about your name?" I say my name is long and hard for the people to say, and that the people might not like my name. He says then to put the name of my business. I say it has no name. Make up a name, he says. I think of my old uncle. I say, "Five," but then I think I got to make it so even my old uncle would have to laugh. "Six!" I give the printer the same kind of look my uncle gave me. The printer doesn't care about the look I give him, or, after, ask me what it means when I say, "Six Quarters."

::

I don't think my wife ever tells me the same story twice. I tell her the same two stories now many times. I tell her the five quarters one, and she asks me questions. I can answer because it is my story. The other one I tell is one that I only heard, so she doesn't ask questions. But I think she likes it just as much.

You know, the way I answer your question is maybe different than I tell it before. Same story, but I take longer, put in a little more. Lots of things are different now. People on the other sides of doors. Sure. Two kids: little boy, baby girl.

My wife reads the little boy books—reads him books! So now I listen, like I am a little boy. Me! I don't say anything, but I listen to those books and I change my stories. When I tell her my aunt's story now, I start off, "It was a long, long, time ago." She laughs. But it was a long, long time ago when my old uncle first sees my aunt.

"My old uncle was old when he got married. He would go north and work—Texas, California, Idaho, as far north as North Dakota. No drinking, no smoking, no restaurants. Maybe some bread, some tomatoes; maybe he sits by himself by a river. And once a year, in the spring, he would come back to the village. He was getting older, and no wife."

I stop the story there for a while. I say to my wife, "*It was a long, long time ago.* Maybe before hairdressing schools and before hairdressers made more money than guys who can pay just for baby-sitting and day-care doing small engine re-pair." She smiles at me. Then I start the story again.

"So he rides back into town on a horse. A horse is what people had there in those days. Even just to look at a car was a big thing. And to ride in one? So he comes into town on his horse, and everybody knows about it, that he was away in the north working, and no wife. You know, in Mex-ico at that time almost any woman over nineteen years old —married. Had to be. Maybe you find one or two eighteen, a few more seventeen, not married—maybe. Maybe sixteen you had some to pick from. And the mothers are dressing up their daughters, pushing them at him. But my uncle doesn't say anything. It looks like he will ride out of town like every year—not married. Except he is riding down a street one day, and he sees a girl playing jacks. You know, bouncing a ball, picking up jacks. Out in front of her house; for something to do. And she looks up at him, on the horse.

It's a small town, so he would pretty much know who she is —just a poor girl. He goes over into Texas for a day and he buys her a nice dress. When he comes back into town, he goes to her house, talks to her parents, and they call her in. And he gives her the dress. He didn't say anything to her and she didn't say anything to him, but as he leaves town on his horse the next day, she watches him go. When she can't see him anymore, she climbs up a ladder onto the flat roof of the house. For another minute or so, she can see him. Then she looks around for the highest building in town with a roof. So she can watch him some more. And she comes down the ladder and runs to that building and up the stairs to the roof. And watches him again until he is gone out of sight."

I stop for a minute. I tell my wife, "*My uncle was not a usual man.* Even then, when she was thirteen and he was thirty-three, it was not impossible that he could, in those days, have married her." Then I start the story again.

"Every spring, he comes back to the village on the horse. He would give the family some money so she could have a few nice things. The one day he would come to her house, they would only for a moment look at each other. When they would pass each other somewhere in the town, again that is all they would do—just look at each other. But as he left town every year, there she would be, up on the roof of the tallest building in town, trying to see him for as long as she could, watching him until he was gone out of sight."

Every time I tell it, I stop here. "*This is a true story,*" I tell my wife. Then I start it again.

"When she was seventeen, that spring, he didn't come. He sends some money, and a note to her parents. It says something like, Have her finish grade 11. Let her take grade 12. Something like that."

I stop the story again. "A true story," I say again to my wife.

"So he didn't come that spring, and he didn't come the next spring, but then in the summer he comes. In a car—a car!

"It was a car like they don't make anymore, with a two-stroke, like a lawn mower, an outboard, a motorcycle engine. To him it must have been music. And they drove away together, to get married, over into Texas."

::

My wife, she never asks me too much about that story of my aunt's. But the one with the five quarters, because it is my story only, she asks: What was the sky like? What was the air like? What was the ground like? What was the rose like? How did my old uncle, how did he smell the rose?

But you know, I'll tell you something. If I leave for work in the morning before she does, she stands in the window up in the apartment and waves to me. I cross the street and walk a little way up the street to the corner. Around the corner is where I park my car. She waves to me as I walk. With one arm she holds the baby girl, and with the other she waves. The little boy, he is standing next to them. Like my wife, he is waving, and he is also saying, all the time, "Daddy Daddy Daddy. Daddy Daddy Daddy."

Now, it is not exactly like in my old aunt's story—my wife doesn't go up to the roof so she can see me a little longer. But at the corner I turn around to see them, and that's when she says out the window, between the Daddy Daddy Daddys, "Call me." We talk already a lot by that time of the day, you know, and before that—the day before, after work and in the night. But still that's what she says: "Call me."

That's why I look down at my watch so much whenever I'm working. I see when she's between appointments, I leave the lawn mower alone for a minute, I wipe my hands, I say,

"My wife's between appointments, can I use my phone?" Like I say to you now, my wife's between appointments, can I use my phone?

I use my phone. I call her.

QUIET

Best, she likes to play things by Ysaÿe, the Belgian violinist and composer. Ysaÿe liked Bach the best. She likes Ysaÿe, then Bach.

Bach didn't play violin, but the sonatas he wrote for it are the most beautiful. They say Bach was the bridge between the old and new music; listening to Ysaÿe's music, you know he knew that about Bach.

Even before she touches the bow to the strings, she knows that Ysaÿe's music is a bridge between Bach and her violin, and that, when she starts to play, the music will be a bridge between her violin and herself.

So she plays in her funny way—letting her shoulder go as much as she can and tilting her head more than other violinists do. In order to hold the violin as far back as possible, to get its sound as close as she can to her ear.

It's a wonder she doesn't have an off-center, sideways kind of look—not only from the way she plays the violin, but also from moving her head around so much, trying to see what people say. Trying to hear.

But she doesn't look any the worse for it; she's good looking. And blond hair. And blue eyes. And breasts that rest nicely on the rib cage. No, she looks good. And she talks OK. And she plays the violin well. She plays it very well.

Never in bed, but always when she plays the violin, she wears a rubber band in her hair, to hold it behind her, so it doesn't get in the way. And she takes off her earrings when she goes to bed, and when she plays violin, but the rest of the time she leaves them in. Her mother had her ears pierced when she was just one or two.

She knows it's nobody's fault, and that one thing had nothing to do with the other, because it was this way for her since she was born; they just didn't figure it out for a while that with one of her ears she could hardly hear, and with the other, she couldn't, not at all, hear.

::

Ysaÿe had an unusual way of holding the bow—she doesn't think anyone really knows why he held it that way, just three fingers and a thumb, the little finger off by itself, angled into the air. He could hear OK; he didn't hold the violin like she does, way far back. But that's how she started using just three fingers holding the bow, because with her right forearm reaching around so far, keeping her little finger also pressed down seemed to make her wrist tired.

When you play Ysaÿe, you get to play Bach too, because Ysaÿe liked Bach's music so much he'd put little recognizable bits of it into his own.

When she plays violin, because she plays solo violin, she never plays Vivaldi. Vivaldi could play violin, but he wrote for so many instruments in so many ways, he didn't spend much time writing things for just one violin at a time. And Paganini—Paganini was such a good player that it's hard for anyone who's not a virtuoso to really do justice to the greatest things that he wrote. But Ysaÿe wrote his best things specifically with individual violinists in mind; Ysaÿe's things, she could play all night.

::

Solo violin. Really, solo only. Having someone accompany her on the piano—maybe. But solo violin with no piano is easier for her.

Her in a string quarter? It wouldn't work. Almost as unlikely as her in an orchestra—without a hearing aid, she couldn't really hear the others playing, but with one, it would be a mess. Because a hearing aid isn't very useful to her when there are a lot of sounds around—it brings them all up at her, each with nearly the same loudness; she wouldn't be able to listen to all those sounds and hear herself play.

But at least she's always had the latest in hearing aids, ever since her parents found out she couldn't hear well. She still has the first one in a drawer, the one she started wearing when she was two and a half. So she's always been hearing something, either that way or through special earphones hooked up to tape recorders and record players, things like that. Out in the world, though, whether her hearing aid's in or out, if she's talking to people, the way it's best for her is one person at a time. And it's the same with dancing—she couldn't really enjoy going out to a dance, because, with a hearing aid, there are too many sounds, and without one, it's really not possible to hear the music and talk and have fun.

::

She started a long time ago with boys. Just talking. Maybe kissing. "I'll ask you a question in your ear and you answer in my ear," she'd start. Then, "Do you think I'm prettier than…?" And she'd say the name of a girl she thought was the fifth-prettiest in her class at school. And the boy would always give the same answer: "Yes."

And then she'd ask the question again but with the fourth-prettiest girl's name.

"Yes."

And it would go like that until she said, "So I must be the prettiest."

"Yes." And then he'd get a kiss.

Later, she would get them to hum into her ear while dancing. She would hum in a boy's ear while he hummed in hers. Because it was really the only way that she felt sure of herself when she was moving with somebody else to music. For her, it was the only good way, but for anyone it's a good way to dance. So without any other music than that, the boy and her would be dancing; the older she got, the more places that led.

Her parents weren't hearing-impaired. She's glad they helped her in the ways that they did, with the doctors and the hearing aids and the special classes and the music lessons, but even though her parents helped her, after a while she didn't much feel like listening to them. As she got older, their voices got fainter and fainter to her, until, like today, she's as good as deaf to anything they say.

When she got married, they thought she was finally starting to listen to them again, because she was doing something they wanted. Afterward, she would sometimes think that's the way it was, too—but no, really no, it wasn't that way. Anything she'd ever done, she wanted to do. And sometimes the things she was doing—she knows she got pretty wild. But she just wanted to know, to let herself know, she was alive.

So for a while she didn't care about talking, not more than anything else. Then she narrowed her life down and narrowed it down. And, as she did, she guesses she calmed down. Because she decided what she needed was a man who would talk into her ear. Not just the slow words and short sentences that he might say to her at night, but all kinds of things, before, and after, and the rest of the day, whenever he was around her. Someone who'd bring the world in a little closer. So everything wouldn't seem so remote.

When you can't hear very well, you often miss fine points. The trailing-off of some things, the leading-into of others: their directions, where they are going or come from. You hear something said, and later you may say exactly the same thing, but you say it too directly, or not directly enough. Because when you heard it you were concentrating so hard on just getting the words you may not have been able to also pick up on just how it was said. She thinks this might take away from what you say. From what you do.

But even if she'd had perfect hearing, when it came to those things she might have said or done to avoid being alone, she doesn't know if she would have said or done anything very different.

::

Besides the violin lessons, she took classes in lip-reading, hand-spelling, and sign. Hand and sign, she doesn't use them too much, since being able to hear a little has kept her mostly in the hearing world. Still, they're good to know. Other ways to talk. And she would feel silly if she came across a deaf person and they couldn't communicate. Lip-reading she does all the time. She really has to. To fill in what she doesn't hear.

So the violin, lip-reading, hand, and sign—but what wasn't easy to learn was the Helen Keller thing. You know, being deaf and blind, at first Helen Keller could only do the manual alphabet, letter by letter on the hand, but then she learned how to speak to people by touching their lips and faces and feeling the vibrating of sounds in their throats as they spoke; then putting her fingers on her own face, lips, and throat until she got everything right.

It wasn't really something that made sense for herself to do, because even if she closes her eyes so she won't see someone's lips, if she's near enough to reach out and feel the sounds in that person's throat, she can hear them anyway. Hear them with one ear, even with her hearing aid out. She could cover that ear with her other hand so she wouldn't hear anything, and concentrate on the vibrating, but she knows from trying that if she does that, it's like being all the way deaf, and she get frightened. Very frightened.

Of course, Helen Keller was using her fingertips to learn how to speak, and she already knows how to speak. But Helen Keller was first learning how, with her fingertips, to listen, and how could she herself be happy with herself unless she started doing at least that?

::

She had a few violin teachers. None that were so special and none for too long. She was kind of a wary student; she didn't know if she really wanted to learn or really wanted to not learn. To deliberately not learn, as if there were some responsibility in learning to play. And she was unsure as to why she chose the violin, except that there aren't many instruments where the sound is so close to your ear. As she got more self-confident, though, she could sometimes relax —if you relax and move your feet as you play, it's almost as if you were dancing with someone humming into your ear.

If she plays what would sound loud to other people, it sounds just medium-loud to her. Because she's not used to hearing sounds even that loud. So she plays what would be medium-loud to other people, and, for her, that's just what she needs. She can hear it; the sound goes right into her ear, but to her it doesn't sound medium-loud. To her it sounds quiet.

The minute she gets home from work, the very second she gets into the apartment, she takes her hearing aid out. And she doesn't put it back in again until she leaves the next day. She knows, out there in the world, it's a good thing to have; she accepts it. But there is, and always has been, for

her, like glasses might be to kids who can't see well, some-
thing foreign about it. When she was little, she knew she
needed to wear it, so she did, but then she refused to wear
anything she thought she didn't need. Like bracelets, or
necklaces, or rings. She didn't even want a watch. And she
wouldn't wear combs, or clips, just a rubber band sometimes
to hold back her hair.

But, before long, she was wearing all of that, and more.
A woven thing on her ankle. Fine gold chain around her
waist. Rings on six fingers.

Now she just wears the earrings, and just one ring. And a
rubber band to hold back her hair.

::

If she had been born all the way deaf, she wonders, how
would she have found this feeling she sometimes has now.
The first time she heard it, it was as if there was another
person in the room, telling her what she was feeling. And it
was a new feeling for her—so new it was almost a new
word.

Not that there's not lots of anger in some violin music:
there is, but you usually expect it. It's called for, like sweet-
ness. But one time when she was playing something by
Ysaÿe, a sweet part, there it was—something beneath the
sound, something trying to come through. And when she
came to the angry part, it sounded so full that it was as if
her violin was playing to her, playing a word and a feeling.

::

Lately she's been thinking of getting pregnant. Except
then she thinks, what if it's born like her. Someone might
grow up wanting someone who—but no, she still doesn't
think it's too much to ask of someone, to talk into your ear.

When he proposed, she told him that's what she wanted most. To have someone who would always do that. To fill her in on all the things she might have missed hearing. To make up for lost time. And to keep her from missing any more things.

"You bet," he said. He said it all moist right into her ear. She heard it and felt it. "You bet." He said it and said it.

So during the ceremony she thought for sure he would say "You bet" instead of "I do." She really thought he would. And when he didn't and it came time to kiss the bride, she thought for sure that was when he was going to do it, to say "You bet" into her ear. It would have been nice. She doesn't like to complain, but it would have been nice.

::

Whenever she plays the violin, she takes off her earrings. She takes off the one from the ear she can hear with, the one closest to the violin, even if it's not a dangly one that might swing against the violin as she plays. She doesn't want anything between her and the violin when she plays.

And she takes off the other earring, too, even though it's not really in the way. Even if it made any kind of sound, it wouldn't matter. Because it's on the ear that can't hear. But she takes it off. To treat it the same as the ear that can hear. To be fair.

Before she gets into bed, and before she plays the violin, that's when she takes off her earrings, but only before she plays the violin does she take off her ring. It's not that it would get in the way when she's playing, and it's not that she takes any ring off her other hand, because she wears only one ring now. But she takes it off. To be fair. To be fair.

::

She's playing two rooms away from him. If there was anything moist about her, it's evaporated into the room, unless maybe there's some sweat trapped between her rib cage and breasts.

Sometimes she edges the bow high up on the fingerboard, like they say Ysaÿe did. And that does give a good sound, a resonating sound.

She hears high-pitched tones better than low-pitched ones. All violinists would agree: you hear and you feel the music you play. But when she says that, it means only the higher notes. The lowest notes, she just feels.

She doesn't have any earrings on. No earrings, no necklace, no bracelets, no fine gold chain at the waist, and around her ankle, no woven thing.

And it's quiet. In the middle of the night their apartment can get so quiet it's like what it must be like to be all the way deaf. And she can get frightened. Very frightened.

Even if she's there in the middle of the day, because of how little she can hear, she forgets that it's not really so quiet. In the day, if she wants to remind herself how noisy it actually is, she just has to look out the window.

But in the middle of the night she knows it's quiet. By looking, by the light of the streetlight. On this street at three in the morning, she's more likely to find moonlight than car lights. Yes, it's quiet; she can see that it is.

She can see that it is, but if she really wanted to be sure, she'd just stop playing, lay down the bow and do the Helen Keller thing. Put her fingertips against the window. Because, if there's any sound outside, it vibrates into the glass. If there's any sound out there, her fingertips could tell.

So all she'd have to do now to be sure that it's quiet is to stop playing, lay down her bow, and touch her hand to the window. Except she doesn't want to stop playing.

But it's quiet. You bet. You bet. Violin quiet.

BORN HERE

"Parish me no parishes."
—Peele, *The Old Wives' Tale*

"Thank me no thankings, nor proud me no prouds."
—Shakespeare, *Romeo and Juliet*, Act III, sc. 5

"Vow me no vows."
—Beaumont and Fletcher, *Wit Without Money*, Act. IV, sc. 4

"O me no O's."
—Ben Jonson, *The case Is Altered*, Act V, sc. 1

"Cause me no causes."
—Massinger, *A New Way to Pay Old Debts*, Act I, sc 3

"Front me no fronts."
—Ford, *The Lady's Trial*, Act II, sc. 1

"Petition me no petitions."
—Fielding, *Tom Thumb*, Act. I, sc. 2

"But me no buts."
—Aaron Hill, *Snake in the Grass*, sc. 1

"Play me no plays."
—Foote, *The Knight*, Act II

"Clerk me no clerks."
—Scott, *Ivanhoe*, Chap. 20

"Diamond me no diamonds! ... Prize me no prizes."
—Tennyson, *Idylls of the King*

Isabel, Sucia, Ola, then me, Americo—Americo because I was born here—then the twins. Not that the folks didn't know that where they came from was also America, like on maps, all the way up and down, it's America. But here, on the mainland, how it must have been for them the first years was: Finally, America! And finally a boy.

I really don't go for photographs, not too much, but that one looks good on the dash. You like this Batmobile? As the guy on the lot told me, "This vehicle, it belonged to a minister upstate, all it needs is that one bit of work you can see." I was about to tell him that I'd never been upstate, and to keep his black car.

But then it felt good to sit in—so you like it? Excuse the forest-green fender which I picked up out by Shea. I've got a spray can to paint it.

Anyway, you can see that that's an old picture—the photographer who came around lined us up according to height, or age, I forget which, but at the time it was the same. So Isabel, she went all the way through high school and was going to go up to City College that fall, but then she took her first trip down to the island that summer and phones from there to say she wants to get married. So Ma-mi went down and watched her get married. And the next year, pictures of her baby started to come up, and since Sucia was always as one with big sister, as was Ola with Sucia, within a few years they were also down there and married, and with the little ones. Then Ma-mi and the twins went ahead, down there to live, while Pa-pi sold the store. When he left, I traded our big upstairs apartment for the basement one—it's not so bad. It's below ground in the front but opens in the back to a bit of a yard. For the summer I rigged up a shower out there.

I really only started reading books after the folks left. Right away I thought maybe I should have a system for it, so I go alphabetically by author, one book by one author. The first time around I was reading the books everyone knows, so when I was in the A's it was *Pride and Prejudice*.

What is happening to me now might be because of my reading. It's not that now I don't—I do, I still believe in the body, but where I used to think, Americo, find yourself someone from the neighborhood, something like you know, now it's Americo, you've got to find something different for yourself, someone like you don't even know you don't know.

Of course, not all of my ideas come from books. Just like before, when the folks left, I could have gone with them, but I figured, me, Americo, I was born here, I'll stay. And that I'd find something to do, even for a little while, and buy myself some kind of car. That was an idea all my own. I still get them.

Now, if it was cold today, I would just sit in the car in the sun somewhere and read, but when it's warm enough like this, I drive up to go read in the park. And best is that it's not a factory town, not our city. Every minute somebody's got a different reason for moving a car, I don't worry about parking.

So as close to Seventy-second Street as possible, to walk in on the path to the right of the road there. Up past the Bandshell, then down the steps and over to where the grass slopes off to the Lake, that's before you get to the Boathouse. You see those people out there in the rental boats? As some philosopher said, they think they're having fun and they are. You like my island, all of two feet from shore? It's the only rock here that's big enough to sit on while keeping your feet dry. Today's book is *Mansfield Park*.

::

You've got to be careful where you read a book. This rock's a good place—it's outdoors, but with the trees leaning in like they are, it's enclosed, almost like indoors. I could never read up at the Great Lawn between the Eighty-fifth and Seventy-ninth Street transverses. All that sky. Last time I walked through there I caught myself mumbling. "Life could be beautiful." Because of the way that the space is so open there. For reading, it would be worse—you'd close the book thinking, wasn't it great, that the whale didn't get Ishmael.

::

It was only a plan, you can't always get too far with a plan. At least you shouldn't start believing too much in the picture of it, the one you put in your head as you ask your question. Because a question can get answered with questions: "Fun?" "How is it fun?" And maybe you will or won't try to say why it's fun to take some coffee and go downtown to the West Side by the Hudson and spend the afternoon sanding and painting the fender. That it's fun like an outdoor shower is fun unless you can't see that it is. So you ask your question and the answer you get gets rid of your question, gets rid of your plan, but still you can't get rid of the picture.

::

I was opening a bank account for my T-shirt business, and I don't know how the form put it, but what the man asked was, "Parents?" So I said, "They're in Puerto Rico." Then he said, OK, but what he meant was living or dead. And I thought, yeah, Puerto Rico, if I stay here and they stay there, it'll always be like a third thing for me.

::

It did, but now it doesn't surprise me how many people don't see the bat. They see the yellow, which looks like an upside-down crocus with its leaves reaching up to it. Some people get pretty angry: "Bat?" "How is it a bat?" And what should I say? Maybe, "Mister, to you, it's the Sign of the Crocus!" Or, "Lady, you must know Crocusman!" What should I say? And will it matter, whatever I say?

Like right now, it's not just that your eyes do or don't see the bat on my T-shirt—it's your mind that's seeing just one thing at a time, bat or crocus or bat. And, on the weekends, that's seeing my stand full of T-shirts and not seeing me, Americo, seeing you seeing or not seeing the bat.

But some days what even I see is the crocus and then I have to turn my own mind around to start seeing the bat. Me, Americo. And those are my T-shirts!

::

I always worked weekends. It was interesting, growing up around the store, people coming and going. And it was a real grocery store, not a bodega, bigger, but not a supermarket either. Smaller, a grocery store.

It's still there, and run by a family. Sometimes when I walk by it, especially at night, what I see is a play in which just the faces are new. I could go in, they don't know who I am, or even if they did, I could, but why? Now if I need something, I go to a bodega, or a supermarket.

::

When the twins worked the two side-by-side cash registers for Pa-pi after school while they were finishing junior high, they still looked alike to me. When one of them started to paint her fingernails red I thought they still looked alike, except for that. Even the way they pressed their fingers against the buttons on the registers, even that looked alike.

Isabel, Sucia, Ola—it's no excuse, but when you're growing up and have three big sisters, you don't always get to be much of a brother. And the twins had each other. So when I went into the back room at the store that day and saw the twin who wasn't painting her fingernails sitting there on the floor, sideways to the wall, knees gathered up and face into them, crying, I didn't know what to say. I looked above her, at the shelves where the twins when they were younger used to crawl up into the empty spaces and take naps there together. They were small, the twins.

Then, not only for something to say, but also because I thought there might be something to know, I started to tell her, "Look, I don't really understand why one girl paints her fingernails and one doesn't—" when she turned her head and looked right at me through dark hair and tears and said like she wanted me to learn something, "Because."

Even if she didn't say any more to me then, or really much to anyone after that before leaving for Puerto Rico, I was up all the way to one minute in my life when I had someone to talk to, and now I'm always thinking that the next minute could come any minute.

She's the only one with the folks now since the other twin met some guy and moved to Florida. If I call Puerto Rico and the twin at home answers, she says, "How are you, Americo," and gives the phone to Pa-pi, who says to come visit, that the coconuts fall and you drink the milk from a straw, and that at night the guys play drums around fires on the beach. Then Ma-mi takes the phone and says that because the ocean there is the same temperature as the air, you can't tell without looking which part of your body is in or out of the water, and that the flowers she grew on our bathroom windowsill in New York grow wild everywhere on the island. The twin never takes back the phone. If I call and the twin answers and she's the only one there, she says, "How are you, Americo," that Ma-mi and Pa-pi aren't there, to call back when they're there.

::

"Miracles me no miracles." I don't know how John Bartlett missed it. I spotted it right away, it was fresh in my mind because B comes before C.

After all, Bartlett had other things from *Don Quixote*. There was: "He had a face like a benediction." "Every one is the son of his own works." And something about sleep covering you like a cloak, that it was "heat for the cold and cold for the hot." I remember that. He even had stuff from another book by Cervantes, *La Gitanilla*, "The Little Gypsy," which I get to read soon.

Even though Bartlett had a different translation than I did, how different could it have been? The miracles thing in Spanish might be "No me milagres," but it's probably just "Milagro mi no milagros."

I know—in Spanish, Milagros is also a girl's given name. I don't know anyone by that name, but I can miss things I can't even remember and people I don't even know I don't know. Anyway, you can't go by names, you get surprised. Just like the three little words that you hear might not be the ones you're expecting, the ones you could want for the long run.

::

The best thing for New York is a poor memory," that's what we say in this city, that's what you need here to live. Otherwise you'll walk around with your face out of shape all day about what happened last week, or yesterday, or this morning. It's like there's only so many streets and you can't avoid all of them, so what we use as a prayer here is, "Forget about it."

But now, about me, Americo, two feet from shore: As you can see—shoes barely wet. Socks not wet. Those clouds in the sky, there, through the leaves—life could be beautiful, isn't it so? And really, wasn't it great that Ishmael got away? So *que pasa*, Austen Jane? For today, enough of our garden? Then, "To the Batmobile," as we say in my country. "Back to the Batcave."

FEELING MARLENE

DEAR ED,

I'm writing to you from a hotel room in Atlanta.

This hotel has passed for home for me for the last nine or ten months. I've been working here as an instructor in industrial design in a pilot project set up by the state of Georgia. They say I'm pretty good at teaching, so I guess it's true.

I got your card in the mail via my ex-wife in Saskatoon. On it you wonder where I am, if I am still writing, and if I have any stories I would send for you to look at because you think I should be published, too.

You ask also about whatever happened to the untitled novel I showed you over gin a long time ago in Montana and you wanted to take with you, the one, as you think you remember, "where the guy on the West Coast gets drunk, staggers from side to side over the British Columbia-Washington state border and has an identity crisis as to whether he feels more Canadian or American."

The problem is itchy feet. That's what Iris (older daughter) says. It's hard to get control of your life if you have them. By the time you get this letter I will be on my way to another place. This is the story:

1. I have this girlfriend. She is pretty young (thirty), and wants to move in with me and get married. She's a great

woman with a great name (Deirdre). Most of the time I think it's a good idea.

2. Next week I leave here and fly to Winnipeg to pick her up. We're driving to Idaho to attend a fiftieth wedding anniversary of my parents. We'll be there until the end of October.

3. In November I'll be in Detroit for a few weeks, waiting to go to my new job. After that I'll be off to Papua New Guinea for the better part of the year. There are two electricity-generating plants being built. I'll be the Head-Coordinator for both. This sounds like something with potential.

I don't have an address for PNG as yet. I guess I'll get that when I get there. I have your address in my wallet. I liked the picture on your postcard, with those three Atlantic Canada fishermen holding the cod. I'm going to send you one like that, which I'm sure they must have in New Guinea, but the fishermen, and even the fish, are bound to look much, much different.

It has been interesting living here in a major American city, but it hasn't been interesting enough. Where I was living in Ottawa was more exciting, really. I strongly recommend Elgin Street in Ottawa. Sometimes I think I made a mistake. After I left GM and worked in Sweden and came back, I went to Ottawa-Hull because it was so interesting. Where I was living there on Elgin was downright mysterious —they called it Little Lebanon. Even though everyone could speak English—and Parisian French—they loved it when I'd throw in a few words in Arabic, which I'd picked up when I consulted on that desalinization plant in Bahrain. The Canadian government also wanted to give me a six-month contract to oversee the construction of an irrigation system in Cuba, but because I am a U.S. citizen, I began to wonder if I might not get in some trouble doing that, possibly from the Cuban direction, but more likely from the American one. Were I braver, I might have concentrated on my original plan, which was to stay put on Elgin Street and write up some things. Consulting in engineering was to be a way to pay the bills, but it took over. This is not unfortunate, since I like building things and teaching about it. Nevertheless, I suspect I might have regrets later on.

Are you doing any writing? I ask that with trepidation, since in my brief phone conversation with your ex in New Haven last year, I got the impression that your attitude toward your writing was complicated, and not an area where an outsider should venture. Maybe I'm reading my own attitudes into your situation. When I let people read what I write they usually say that it's good. I think it's poorly executed, and that I should stick to consulting. I admire your courage.

I wrote "Feeling Marlene." An interesting old lady, obsolete, smokes a cigarette after her meal, like Marlene Dietrich. I wrote "Murder by Mathematics," where a lonely professor kills rivals on his personal computer. In "Clown Bandits," Bozos terrorize Ontario, the last place on earth with white people working in 7-Elevens. "Famous Apples" was about a poor fellow unable to adapt to growing Delicious. "Español" was about an unfortunate rich guy who was transferred to Montreal, hit on the head by a foul at an Expos game and emerged fluent in Spanish but unable to distinguish it from French. And so forth. When I move, the stories usually get lost.

Almost everybody in your stories is pretty whole. At first they seem disconnected, but they aren't. That's a good thing.

How is Prince Edward Island? I miss the wild blueberries. Sometimes I miss the way of life there.

As you can guess I have a computer and a little printer. What do you think of that? I wonder why anyone needs all this stuff. **All the different fonts.** I really don't know much about these things. People tell me computers are wonderful.

Atlanta has been nice enough, and I suppose I'll look back fondly on the city. I should be returning to teach for several weeks each year. Edith (other daughter) has graduated from the University of Toronto and opted to take an entry-level position at a think tank in Virginia. I don't expect it to last too long, frankly. In some respects I've set a poor example. Iris is currently with Canada World Youth, in Western Africa for the second time. She's married.

I apologize for not writing you sooner. Were there an excuse, I would offer it. It was really nice to hear from you. I'll write again from New Guinea and let you know if that particular Paradise is all they've made it out to be.

You'll hear from me soon. Promise.

Bobby

THREE POINT BACK

"So when's Paul coming back?"

Tracey always asks Evan this, about every day for two weeks now, and the answer he gives and has given since after the first or second time is what he hopes will keep her from asking again. "I. Don't. Know.."

"Well then *is* he?"

"Tracey...."

"You call him? Or he calls you at work, right? He's got you keeping secrets from his wife, and me too?"

"I don't know *where* he is; I don't know when he's coming back, *if* he's coming back."

Some days that ends it for the day. But there are other days.

"He was pointing at *you*, Evan."

"He was just *pointing*. At the wall. He wasn't even looking where he was pointing."

"Evan, he was signaling you."

"Now, look. Donna herself hasn't asked me, not even once. And you—"

"Donna wasn't home yet."

::

Donna wasn't home yet from some meeting and Tracey and Evan had just been driving around and stopped without calling. Evan rang the lit button on the back door.

"It's open."

Paul was sitting at the dining room table. No book, no magazine, no food. And no radio on, or TV; nothing. A clear, shiny wood table. Twilight outside, and no lights on in.

"Just waiting for Donna to show up?" Tracey had asked, though it didn't need asking. "Kind of *still* around here, Paul. Silence is one thing—or maybe you don't like music anymore?"

Paul didn't answer.

"But you should have something *moving* around here." Tracey looked around, then said, "Paul, you should get a cat."

Paul did answer that. At first he just shook his head, but then he said, "A cat. No, I don't think so. It's not..."

"Get one and see," Tracey said. "Paul, you *like* cats. I've seen you around them—you like cats."

Paul hadn't looked at Tracey when he'd answered. And he still didn't when he pointed and said, "Point at a cat..." And he wasn't looking at where he was pointing either, as he said that, because he was looking at the other curling fingers of his hand, and sort of wiggling them while he said, "And three fingers point back."

He and Evan and Tracey sat there a moment. Paul didn't say anything else; Evan hadn't felt there was any more to say —he suddenly thought it was kind of nice sitting there at the empty table, the three of them, now each not alone, and sharing that silence and stillness. But then Tracey said, "At a cat?"

Paul didn't say anything. But Tracey wouldn't let up. "Paul," Tracey said, "are you saying you're a cat?"

::

Paul would never have said that, Evan knew. Because he finds Paul always says just enough, or maybe less than enough, but never more—unless, Evan learned, you got him off guard. Especially if you weren't even trying. One Saturday down at the outdoor handball court, Paul had been playing straight-out for one hour, two hours, three hours.

"Don't you ever get tired, Paul?"

Evan meant tired at handball. Paul looked through the chain-link sides of the court and started to say, "Yes, I...," but then he looked back at Evan and said, "Oh, you mean in *here*. No, in here, I don't hold myself back."

When Evan told Tracey about it, she said, "Paul's crazy —he thinks that's what makes someone tired, holding back? What about before, when he was holding *out*? He got tired that way too. He should count himself lucky to have what he's got, including Donna."

Then, at the table, Paul didn't have to say a thing, but Evan knew he would, because Paul was always, finally, accommodating. So Paul told Tracey about a woman with a secondhand store who would take in and find homes for stray cats. He brought her one he found in a vacant lot. She said she'd take it if he'd take her and the cat to the vet. And at the vet, when they asked what the cat's name was, the woman said, "The cat's name is Paul."

Paul said whenever he'd see the woman anywhere, he'd say, "How's Paul?" Until one time she said, "Paul's not called Paul anymore. Got a home. And the people who get my cats like to give them new names."

Evan thought Paul telling Tracey that was a good way of answering, but to let Tracey off a hook can be to put yourself back on one. "Paul," she said, "why didn't *you* keep the cat?"

So then Evan took Paul off the hook by saying the first thing he really said while sitting there. Doing what Paul had just done, one finger pointing off with the lower three curling round, Evan said, "Point at a cat...."

::

That night, they'd got to Paul's at seven fifteen. They'd left him at a quarter to eight. And it was getting dark then. They got home at ten after. At eight thirty, Donna called. "Where's Paul?"

The first day after, Tracey started saying how Paul should have waited. "He could have sat for another forty-five minutes."

Evan started telling her how time can start to seem long. That maybe Paul wanted to be held. Felt he needed to be, say, at 8:04 sharp. "You know, *held*. Like a cat."

But Tracey said, "Sure, *held*. How about *stroked?*"

And Tracey still thinks that the thing Paul did with his fingers was some kind of signal. To Evan, that he'd be leaving. Even though Evan reminds her she's the one who brought it up, about cats. Says it was just Paul's way of telling her a person might ask too much of a cat.

And Evan himself gets home every night a little before Tracey does. It isn't dark then, but it's the end of the day. It gets darker, not lighter. And now, he doesn't turn on the lights. When Tracey gets home, she'll turn on the lights.

When Tracey's not home yet, Evan's started to think about Paul, because two days, O.K.; two weeks, O.K., maybe. But two months? Or two years?

Though Evan can get tired thinking like this, he's starting to learn how to remember exactly the things people say: Say what they said, and do what they did when they said them. When Evan does that, three fingers point back.

AUSTRALIA

Ninalee and her husband Joseph are arguing again. Joseph's sister came to town. Ninalee took her out shopping and bought her a fake designer handbag on a SoHo street corner. But the one the guy let her walk away with for only twenty dollars wasn't quite right—the tiny sewn-on label read **Kate Spad**.

"Kate Spad!" That's what Joseph said later back at their apartment, and he said it while breathing in. Yes, Joseph should hardly be able to control himself, with laughter, Ninalee thinks. But it's rage, and he's only somewhat controlling it. "Sure, sure, it's a big joke to you, here in *sophisticated* Manhattan," he says. "Take her to the real store! Let her buy the real thing—she can afford it. *We* can afford it."

"Kate Spad? Who, Mommy?" That's from Janny. She's five.

"Kate Spad is Andy Spad's wife," Ninalee says. "And Andy Spad has his own store, called Jack Spad—no, *Ack Spad!*" Ninalee really wants to drive Joseph crazy. She crouches down to Janny's level. "Can you say it, Janny?" Ninalee asks. "Can you say *Ack Spad?*"

"Ack Spad!" says Janny. Janny spins around to her little brother, Benjie. He's two. "Benjamin!" she announces. It sounds to Ninalee almost like Atten-shun! "Benjamin," Janny repeats. "Say it. Say Ack Spad!"

"Azz Pazz," says Benjamin, wide-eyed and serious, but

with only a little bit of confidence. If he were older, Ninalee
thinks, he'd probably add, "What's going on?"

::

For a long time now, since Janny was born, Ninalee
doesn't shut the door when going to the bathroom. Ninalee
doesn't want to miss one little thing—good or bad, frighten-
ing or hilarious—that Janny might make happen or have
happen to her. The leaving-the-bathroom-door-open might
have stopped by this time, but of course it had to be ex-
tended due to Benjamin's arrival.

Now it's a long-term goal for Ninalee: when Benjamin is
five, she's going to start closing the bathroom door on him
and his sister. Maybe even locking it. Maybe they'll find
notes from their mother stuck on the outside where Janny
could read them and relay them to Benjamin: "Do not
bother Mommy." "Please do not whine." "Do not ask me
questions through the door." "Do not begin a fight with
each other the minute I go in." "Do not stick your little fin-
gers under the door and wiggle them." "Do not slide me
pennies under the door." "Do not write me messages and
stuff them in under." Whatever Ninalee's future notes will
say, she's conceded to herself they'll have three main ingre-
dients:

"Yes, the door is locked."

"I want you children to be quiet, to stay out of trouble
while I'm in there."

"Yes, yes, yes, I still love you."

::

Because Ninalee never shuts the door, of course Janny
doesn't either. There is a logic to this to Ninalee, but she
doesn't know if it will be so logical to Janny when she's old

enough to think it over. Because her father always closes the bathroom door.

For a while Joseph didn't actually lock it if he was only in there shaving, but now he locks it all the time. And this too is somehow logical to Ninalee: she, Janny and Benjamin on the outside of a door locked by Joseph from the inside.

Ninalee thinks that by the time Janny is eight and Benjamin is five that the change she will make then will make sense to them. What she thinks now that she will tell them then is, "Children, today's the day we—me, you and you—are going to start closing the door when we go to the bathroom." Then she will add, "Like Daddy does."

Does, or did? Used to do? Three years from now, she thinks, he'll still be their father, but where will he be fathering from? A lot could change—she wants a lot to change—in three years.

::

Joseph and Ninalee haven't had sex, or at least any sex she's cared about, for months and months. She imagines it soon will be years, and not too long after that, forever.

After Benjamin was born, they did end up, by mutual agreement, at a marriage counselor. Ninalee made the mistake of telling the woman that she really didn't care about the lack of sex right then, but that only made the counselor, it seemed to Ninalee, more sympathetic to Joseph.

When Ninalee met with the counselor alone, she was informed by her that if they couldn't fix their sex life, well, what was to stop Joseph from looking for one elsewhere? And she gave Ninalee a newspaper article that said, among other things, that during sex with a long-term partner, the heartbeat rate goes from 70 a minute to 120. But if you're having extramarital sex it can go to 180, and some men have heart attacks. Ninalee, reading that, didn't quite giggle, but she did stop going to counseling.

::

Ninalee started looking for someone for Joseph. A woman from far away—as far away as you can get and still speak English. Because it's all going to be hard enough for Ninalee to arrange, and Joseph wouldn't want anything too exotic.

Ninalee's looking for someone who Joseph can't resist—and someone who'll take him home to Mother. Her mother in Canberra. Or Melbourne. Or even New Zealand.

She'd seen ads like that, she's sure, "Lonely Australian woman, young and pretty, on work assignment in New York, looking for local man to show her all the city has to offer…." But, Ninalee thinks, it can't be someone who wants to stay here. If he settled down with someone new in the tri-state area there'd be years and years of shuttling Janny and Benjamin around, Australian step-mom or not.

It has to be someone who wants—and soon—to expose him, long-term, to the outback. Ninalee sees certain promising ads now and then, but in the Escort category: "Saucy Aussie. Just Up from Down Under. Discreet and Discriminating. Does anything. Very expensive. 212…." Yes, Ninalee's seen ads like that—when she sees one again, she's promised herself to write down the number, she's going to make a call. After all, if Joseph was properly motivated, and the woman was, too—different motivations, perhaps—but why not? Yes, why not, thinks Ninalee. He can afford it—we can afford it.

::

Joseph is working from home today, Friday. It really is

too much, thinks Ninalee. Wednesday would be better, because three days in a row—Friday, Saturday, Sunday—with him can be a lot.

Later she'll take the kids outside somewhere, it's a nice day. They'll play in a park, she'll be sitting on a bench. Their daddy will be in his home office in front of his computer. He's in there now, computing away. The door is, of course, closed.

Ninalee, meanwhile, is at the kitchen table making lists of things that have to be bought, and of things that have to be done. One thing—Ninalee doesn't write it down—that really has to be done is making sure about Benjamin. Because Janny is already her mother's daughter, but how to make sure that Benjie is not his father's son?

Now Ninalee gets up from the table. She starts to put some snacks in a bag for Janny and Benjie, and some storybooks in there too, to read to them in the park: books about trains, mostly, and there's one with a bus and one with a car.

No books about planes, though. In very small ways that only an attentive mother with time on her hands can do, she's been suggesting to them that flying in planes isn't something that either would like. It won't come up for a while, but she doesn't want them going off to visit Daddy someday—and really, flying's the only time-efficient way of getting to Australia.

And Ninalee hears Janny right then from the bathroom. "Shit," Janny says. Joseph wouldn't really like hearing that, no swearing in the house, but Janny isn't actually swearing. She's, well, commanding? Maybe coaching? Ninalee knows.

From the kitchen Ninalee can imagine Janny's face now, eyes focused on Benjie, a very serious look on her face as she says it again. "Shit, Benjamin!"

No, it's not swearing—Janny's helping her mother by toilet-training her little brother. He's up on the potty—he'll get it right soon, thinks Ninalee, suddenly completely happy in her own home, while Janny is saying it, again and again, "Shit, Benjamin, shit!"

SATURDAY BIRTHDAYS

Today, in the pizza shop, Johnny almost said "Wow!" about his own mother. When he'd first started helping her all day there back in January, he'd already twice meant to tell her about the boy the summer before last who'd said "Wow!" about her. He'd meant to tell her, but then he'd started to think it would be better to just wait for someone to say it again, and if this time his mother would hear. And then, in the first week of March, even though he was still only eight years old, what he'd figured out was much better: someone loved his mother.

Every Saturday now, after walking with his mother to work, Johnny goes to get fresh basil. The new owners don't really care if there's fresh basil in the pizza sauce, but they're not around on Saturdays anyway.

Before the shop opens for the day, he brings it back and washes it, but his mother likes to chop it herself. And when she's through sprinkling the cut pieces into the tomato-y sauce, his mother runs her hands smelling of fresh basil from her nose to his, and then past it. And week after week she always says the same thing, "It's completely different from dried basil, isn't it?"

Johnny had always wondered why she always says that, and why she always moves her hand past his nose, as if reaching outward. Because when she says it there's no one there up front in the shop at all yet, just him and her. Maybe there's the guys prepping main courses and salads in the big kitchen all the way in the back, but they wouldn't hear.

Why did she always say and do that? At first Johnny had thought maybe it was just one more thing that he didn't understand because he was only eight but that maybe he would when he was nine. Then, as the weeks went by, he had begun to think it might not be necessary to be a whole year older to understand new things—lately, it seemed that even just from Saturday to Saturday he could do that.

::

Since Johnny's father sold the shop, of course the three of them don't drive there and open up early like they used to. But the new owners were glad when his mother offered to keep working on Saturdays if she could. So it had become the new thing for Johnny, walking his mother to work, helping her until the place opened; then he'd go home or go somewhere and find something to do for the rest of the day. That's the way it had gone all last year, but then so many things changed, at least they'd seemed changed to him, from December to January.

That had scared him, on New Year's Eve, when his mother said she wanted to be by herself. There, in the living room, in the dark, smoking a cigarette. He'd never seen her like that. Then he'd spent a lot of time watching her on New Year's Day, and the day after that. And when school started again, he thought it might be a good idea to try to spend more time with his mother. And no one seemed to mind when that first Saturday in January he stayed all day in the shop to help her. Nobody minds still. Of course, he's not getting paid, but he gets his allowance anyway. They do let him keep his tips at the shop, but he always just gives them to his mother to save for him. And since he's started to spend all day in the shop, he's noticed how quickly each

Saturday passes. Each Saturday does, and the weeks between them do—it's already May.

::

On New Year's Eve, Johnny almost told his mother something he thought she should know. About the time the summer before last, when he and his mother and father had gone to a wedding someplace in the country. The people had rented a hall for the reception, and his mother had been dancing and came outside to cool off. On her way to go sit in a lawn chair, she stopped and spoke to him and smoothed his hair back and straightened his tie. After she went and sat down, another guest, an older boy he didn't know, who had been watching, came up to him and asked, "Is that your sister?"

"Sister? That's my mother."

"Your mother?" The boy had then looked over at her. "Wow!"

Johnny hadn't known right away what to think of the boy saying that, but he thought he was glad that his mother hadn't heard. Then, as the boy did, he, too, looked over at his mother in her red-and-white striped dress, sitting by herself in the chair on the grass, under a tree, fanning herself.

How could he let the boy get away with saying something like that, he'd thought, even if the boy was older and bigger. Even if his mother hadn't heard. Then that older boy turned to go into the hall, saying it one more time, but more softly, as if to himself, and shaking his head as he said it, "Wow!" Johnny had stood there thinking and it was almost at the same moment that his father came up behind him that Johnny started to feel glad for his mother, that the boy had said what he did. Johnny had almost told her about it on New Year's Eve, but that would have meant getting out of bed and going into the living room again. He'd decided it would be better to tell her New Year's Day, but when on

New Year's Day things around the house had more or less returned to normal, he didn't want to ruin that by doing or saying anything out of the ordinary, because it might remind his mother of the night before.

When his mother was all dressed up on New Year's Eve, and his father, even though they had tickets for the dance, announced to her he wasn't going to go, Johnny had gone into his room, put on a white shirt, a dark suit, his dress shoes, and a clip-on tie, walked into the living room where his mother was sitting alone in the dark, and said, "I'll take you."

She turned her head and looked over her shoulder at him, then turned it away. "Never mind," she said. "It's all right."

"I'll take you. We can go."

She just shook her head.

"You don't have to dance with me," he pressed on. Even if he was now almost as tall as she was, it was better if he didn't go that far. But someday, he thought, he should get his mother to teach him to dance. "You don't have to dance with me." He said it again. "There'll be plenty of people there you could dance with."

"If I can't dance with my own husband…" That's when he saw, by whatever light was in the room, that her cheeks were wet.

My own husband. He'd never heard her put it like that before. He didn't know why, but he thought it was something he wasn't old enough to hear. He thought about it as his mother thanked him, as he walked back to his room, as he took off his dress shoes and his suit, unclipped his tie, unbuttoned his white shirt, and as he put on his pajamas and got into bed. He didn't stop wanting to do or say something to make his mother feel better. He thought maybe he should go back and tell her about how the boy at the wedding said, "Wow!" about her, or at least he could tell her how nice she looks in that black dress, even if no one else was going to see her in it. He wasn't sure if he stayed awake all the way to midnight, but until he fell asleep he kept thinking for sure that every woman in the world that night was in someone's arms dancing, except for his mother.

::

Johnny woke up on the first day of the year trying to remember another time like that when it might have, but until he'd had to leave his mother alone with tears on her cheeks, smoking a cigarette in the living room in the dark on New Year's Eve, it had never even started to occur to him that his own love wasn't enough for her.

Then, when on New Year's Day, and all through January and February, she seemed O.K. again to him, that was something he just couldn't understand. Not until the first Saturday in March, as his mother was about to put her hand smelling of fresh basil past his nose, with him wondering what he always did, which was why does she always do that, and how can she keep going like she does if his own love isn't enough, did it come to him. As he watched her stir the basil into the sauce while telling him it was time to unlock the door, all of a sudden he couldn't believe that it had taken him two whole months to figure it out, that somebody loved his mother.

By the end of work that Saturday, as the gates were being pulled down, he thought about it and was sure it had to be someone who had been there that day, but who? He was quiet as he walked home with his mother, but he couldn't help just looking at her and smiling now and then. Whenever she smiled back, he thought she looked so different to him now, and that made him more sure.

The next Saturday his own smile was confident and knowing. All day in the shop, it was as if he were in on a pact or a secret. Johnny was hoping his face would say to whoever it was that just because I don't know who you are doesn't mean that I don't know that you do—do love my mother.

Yes, he was sure of it. After all, he himself did, so somebody else could.

::

The difference between February and March became for Johnny like what the difference between New Year's Eve and Christmas Day had been. It was partly because of the way Christmas Day went that he was so confused as he tried to get to sleep on New Year's Eve.

On Christmas, his father wouldn't drive over to her sister's place. "Three hundred days a year I'm tied up with driving," his father had said. His mother didn't say back to him that nobody asked him to put the money he got from selling the pizza shop into the limousine business, or that it was only a couple of miles to her sister's place. She didn't even say, "But it's Christmas."

As Johnny thought about it, he'd noticed for quite a while then that whenever his father was like that, she wouldn't say anything, but just set into motion a way to do what she wanted to do. Even Johnny's putting on his scarf and boots while his mother put on hers that morning seemed to him something that kept life steady, from falling apart and floating away.

A few things surprised Johnny that day. Since it was a long walk to his aunt's place on Henry Street, and he knew his mother wouldn't be much on driving over herself, especially as it had snowed, he was sure she'd call a car service. But she didn't. He and his mother walked. And then she didn't even turn her head at any of the taxis that went by while they walked.

Even before they left the house, Johnny had been amazed to see the coat his mother put on. Her very best coat, one she hardly ever wore. And it was only morning, even if it was Christmas, and she was going somewhere not with his father, but just him, and not someplace fancy, but just her sister's. Johnny had tried not to show his mother any special look on his face when he saw the coat, but whether she did see one or was just speaking more to herself when she said, "I can wear any coat of mine when I want to," he couldn't figure out.

The snow that had fallen through the night made for other surprises. One was that, for a lot of the way that they took, there were no footprints yet, so theirs were the first. Another thing was that, block after block, they never met anybody walking. It *was* early, and it was Christmas; everybody if not in their cars in their houses, he'd guessed.

What a nice walk. For some reason he'd even started flipping the clean dry snow of tree branches and parked cars onto his mother. Onto her best coat. During that walk he'd felt as if she was not only his mother but maybe more, also like what it might be like to actually have a sister. And as much as he did it, his mother let him get away with flipping the snow; she smiled almost as if she was proud of him for doing it.

They had a good time at his aunt's house. All her children were quite a bit older than he was, and there was something about that he liked. And one of them had kids who were quite a bit younger than he, and that was fun too. So he had a good time.

They got a drive back. Then, while his mother got everything ready for their Christmas dinner, he went into the den, where his father was watching TV. Johnny didn't like the show that was on, but he thought he should sit there and watch it, no matter what. Not just because it was

Christmas. "He's your *father*." How many times had he heard his mother say that? "Your father *loves you. You* love your father."

::

When people look at Johnny looking at his mother, he thinks they probably could tell that he does—of course, they can tell that he loves her. But how can he tell who else does? He can't even talk about it with anyone, because he's afraid that would somehow ruin it.

He thinks it's something you learn after a while; after all, it took over two months of Saturdays to figure out that someone loves his mother. Maybe a few more Saturdays and he'll figure out who, he'll get it right.

He doesn't always do everything in the pizza shop right. Sometimes he might hear, "Johnny, you're giving too many napkins." Or, "Johnny, you forgot to give a cup with that Pepsi at table 4." He wonders if anyone notices how he turns his head right and left as he zigzags through the tables. If somebody loves his mother, he thinks, it's got to be someone who sits in a seat facing where she's working. Or maybe that's exactly the opposite of what someone who loves her might have to do. Sometimes Johnny looks at his mother, trying to see if there's some special direction she seems to be looking in. That doesn't help either, but he's sure that sooner or later he'll figure it out.

::

Since April now, they've been letting Johnny take phone orders. Not every kid's birthday is on a Saturday, but it sure seems like that when you help out in a pizza shop, since most of the parties are. Starting early, people phone in orders for pizzas for kids' birthday parties, usually little round mini pizzas, usually plain, and then they drive to pick them up themselves so they get them back to the party at just the right time. Whoever picks them up couldn't be whoever it is that loves his mother, Johnny's sure of that. Because that wouldn't be someone who comes into the shop every Saturday. Still, he's always on his best behavior, even with anyone like that who couldn't possibly be the one, because whoever it is might be in there, sitting at a table, or might come in just when he's helping his mother pack the order. He thinks whoever it is who loves his mother shouldn't have any reasons for not loving him, too.

Johnny used to go to parties like that. Some of the orders he takes are for little kids' birthdays, but some are for friends of his' parties, ones he could have been at. But how could he go to one now and have a good time if he thought he might miss finding out. His mother is always telling him, "Johnny, you should go to a few of those parties." She can't believe it when he says it's more fun being at the shop, but then, he would never say to anyone, especially her, why that's so.

Every once in a while, when there's a lull in the place, Johnny looks around and thinks to himself, It's somebody who is here or was here. After all, how could she do all that she does and put up with what she does unless somebody loves her with as much love as is enough for her?

::

Today, something did happen in the shop, and it had to do with a boy, but not one saying "Wow!" One of the older boys from the neighborhood must have got hold of some wine, and had too much of it, and got into a fight. No one saw who gave him the punch that sent him against the swinging glass door of the shop, which, luckily for the boy, was the kind that opens in.

As he lay there, half in and half out of the shop, Johnny's mother had rushed out from behind the counter and cradled the boy's head and got someone to give her a wet towel. She didn't even seem to care that some blood was getting on her hands and her arms as she wiped his face from his nose to his chin. "Thank you, Mrs...." The boy had trailed off.

As some of the guys there helped the boy up after a while, Johnny noticed blood even on his mother's apron and dress. Then he thought, Maybe this is the time. He looked around at everyone there. Because whoever it is would have the same look as he's sure he has on his own face. He tries that, but either whoever it is isn't there or it just isn't the week when he can figure it out yet.

As Johnny walks home with his mother in the evening, he asks if she knows whether that boy has a mother.

"I don't know, Johnny. I wonder."

"Is he old enough to get married?"

"He's a little young for that, but I suppose he's getting there."

His mother probably didn't know why he was asking so many questions, but he was stringing the answers together for himself. After all, it wouldn't be that many years until he'd be as old as that boy is now. And, also, if that boy didn't have a mother and no one loved him who knew his mother, he'd have to get married to someone who didn't know his mother.

When they got to the house, his father still wasn't home yet. He'd see his father tomorrow. Did he love his father? He'd see. Tomorrow. His father wouldn't be working and, the three of them with Johnny in the back seat, would drive over to his mother's sister's tomorrow.

But it's still Saturday. Even when he gets into bed, there's still some Saturday left. It's Saturday and he's seen who it is, even if he doesn't know who it is.

Even after his mother reaches her arm into the room to flip off the light, it'll still be Saturday, right up to midnight. It's not nearly that late, but he's tired. He starts to think of the boy who said "Wow!" but then he starts to think of he boy who got punched. He begins wondering what it must be like to almost be old enough to get married and to maybe not have a mother. Then to have too much to drink and get knocked down and have blood wiped from your face by someone else's mother.

SOMETHING ABOUT IRELAND

"Come with me, brother, let's take a leak." That was just about the first thing Michael said to me as I came through the swinging doors after clearing customs at Kennedy.

"I just took one on the plane before we started down."

"Then come with me while I take one. Come with me, anyway. Mary'll watch the luggage."

Of course, first he'd introduced me to Mary, his American girl. So earnest-looking she is, and pretty at the same time—not such a bad way for him to ease into the immigrant life.

Inside the washroom, as I started to lean against the long wall opposite the urinals to wait for him, he put his arm straight out and pressed his hand to the tiles by my ear.

"Timothy, she's going to go on about something. She might start in the car on the way in, or at home, or at the restaurant tonight. Because there's something she wants to know, and when she asks you, say that you don't—you don't know."

"About?"

"About Ireland—it's probably what they say over at Galway Bay that she's looking for, what they say about the islands. What Grandfather said to us that time."

"Just that? Michael, it's not much to want to know. And you could tell her yourself."

"But I didn't. Right when I met her, that night when she asked, I told her I didn't know. So now *you* don't know."

After turning and taking a few steps, the same palm he'd leaned on while talking to me he pressed above the urinal on the opposite wall. When he was through, he brought it down on the handle to flush, and turned to walk out.

"Aren't you coming?"

I was still leaning back.

"Maybe I will take one after all. You and this new land have my kidneys at work."

::

Well, most come to stay. They're not coming to look around, or think about it. They say it openly, to themselves and to theirs when they leave their green Ireland. Myself, I just came for a visit to see my own brother, but for most my age on the plane, it's leaving for good. It's the way Ireland works; it's that, not the rain, that's keeping it green—for every one born, one goes away.

Something about Ireland, about islands? Not in the car on the way in, she didn't ask. Not as she made tea for us all as I unpacked my suitcase beside the foam-rubber mattress on the floor that she'd laid out and made up for me.

And not during tea, and not after, when they walked me around to show me the neighborhood, and not that evening at the restaurant they took me to.

And not the next day, Tuesday, when they both got up before me and were off to work, leaving me a note saying we'd all meet at a bar downtown at six.

And it wasn't an Irish bar—in the two weeks I was there, I noticed how my brother, with Mary along, avoided Irish bars; avoided places where anyone just might on the off chance be able to answer one American's question about something Irish.

::

It's true what they say; flying is tiring. I slept late and got up slow at ten in the morning. And not out until noon. Noon in New York, that would be five in the afternoon Dublin time. Then out all day by myself—quite a city. Sharp and fast, yes, but I suppose that if one's willing to put a few old things to the back of the mind and a few new ones up front, that then someone coming from Dublin might stand half a chance.

I found my way to the bar about a quarter hour early. High ceiling and dark clothing; that's probably what everybody new to it must notice about the sleeker bars of New York. This one had a long bar top that came from the wall near the front window and then curved around and went straight and long all the way to the back, except for a break in it, a flip-up sort of thing, about halfway down.

It's in the blood, that between the near section of the bar, which a fellow was tending, and the far, where an attractive young woman was, I'd choose a barstool at the far. But I sat myself close to the break, so it wouldn't be hard for Michael or Mary to spot me from on the bar top than the bartender, she says to me, "You must be Michael's brother. Timothy, right? I'm Ann. He called here to say you'd be coming in, that I should take care of you if you got here early."

"So you know Michael?"

"I know him, and you look like him."

"And you know Mary...."

"I see her when she comes in with him—you really do look like him."

"Well," I said, "we *are* brothers."

Looking at her, I had all kinds of strange thoughts, that

my brother's lonely for family in New York, that he's trying to mate me up with a cute American thing and get me to stay. When neither he nor Mary showed up sharp at six, I thought, they're not coming at all, this woman tending bar's going to take a very drunk me home at closing time. But then Michael and Mary arrived, one on each side of me.

Michael, on my left, says, "Go ahead and ask him, Mary."

Mary says, "Timothy...."

Something about Ireland? I didn't know what to expect. I put my eyes on Michael and, to try stalling Mary a moment, I say, "Here in America, I think I'll go by Tim."

"All right," she says. "Tim. Tim, Michael says that when a female in Ireland says she's going to the washroom, she says, 'I'm going to spend a penny.' Is that true? I never know when to believe him."

"I don't like to admit that anything Michael says is, but this time, Mary, it's so."

"Then," she says, "I'm going to spend a penny."

Mary turned to walk beside the high backs of the barstools to the washroom at the rear. I watched her go, then turned to look at Ann across the bar. But Ann wasn't looking at me; she had her head turned to Michael. And Michael wasn't standing right next to me anymore. He was in the break in the bar, with the flip-up part up and out of the way, behind him. Michael wasn't looking at Ann or me, but watching the washroom door, so, whenever Mary started back our way, he could resume his place beside me. I figured that out when, with no place to look, I just stared down at the bar top—and there were both of Michael's hands, but just one of Ann's. Now, in Ireland, as in America, we can't see through wood, but I'm sure that her other hand was low around the corner of the break in the bar, with Michael pressing against it.

::

Wednesdays Mary had off, so I had two Wednesdays with her showing me around. We were hardly into breakfast on the first one when she began.

"I've been trying to find out something about Ireland—I asked Michael, but he didn't know. I thought you might."

"Something about Ireland?"

"About islands. Something they say in Ireland about islands."

"Well, if you count Ireland as an island I do know one old tale. About an Irish chieftain who returns from what they called then the Unseen Land. To lure his beloved to Ireland, he cries: 'Oh, wouldst thou come along with me to where summer's cool, winters are gentle, spring comes early. Lovely is the island I speak of; here it is as if they young people grow not old. Warm and sweet are our streams that flow, with waterfalls and natural bridges. The notes of birdsong, the flapping of wings are in each glade and thicket. Everywhere softness. Everywhere tenderness. Stop with me. Live with me.' "

Mary said it was a beautiful tale, but the one she was trying to remember wasn't so elaborate. "Mary," I start to say, "I'm afraid I—"

"I think it was more like a saying. It was in a letter I got one time. Where I went to college there was a boy I liked, but he lived with a girl—everybody said they were high-school sweethearts. Maybe I shouldn't have let that stop me, but sometimes I'd be almost ready to say something to him to let him know how I felt, and then I'd think: Don't get between high-school sweethearts.

"Then one day in the mail there was a letter from him. From Ireland, they'd taken a trip to Ireland. When I opened it, at first I just looked at all the words in it—there were probably more there than we'd ever spoken. But when I read it, it didn't seem to be *about* anything. It wasn't about *him*, and not about *them*, and not about *me*. Just all about Ireland. I don't remember much of it, except there was one thing that stood out at the time, something to do with islands.

"I thought to myself, when he gets back, I'll watch—the situation between him and her. After they returned, I did thank him and all, but as far as I could see, things between them seemed the same—high-school sweethearts.

"When college days ended, like everybody else I packed up everything and got on with my life. I came here, met new people. But one day I ran into a woman I knew from then. She was talking about who was where, and she mentioned them—well, who she mentioned was *her*. And what about *him*, I asked. Oh, he wasn't with her anymore, they'd split up the last day of college. She met somebody new, and he just went back to his hometown at first, but then he went by himself to live in Ireland. After a while he met someone there, got married, started a family."

Then Mary says to me, "Tim, I didn't care too much when I heard all that; I mean, I didn't feel it was a big missed opportunity or anything. After that, I even came across the letter he'd sent me. I took the letter from the envelope and just kind of looked at the words without reading it. Then I folded it and put it back in. Because, what did it have to do with me anymore? So I threw it out with a lot of other old things. But the very next day after it was gone, I started to think about it, and was trying to remember some of it. At least the part about islands. It was something the Irish say about islands."

"Mary, why don't you plan to make a trip to Ireland? Maybe you'll see some islands."

"Ireland? Oh, no, I couldn't. I...."

Well, where did Mary and I go that day? The Statue of Liberty, the World Trade Center, Saint Patrick's Cathedral, the Natural History Museum, then back down to meet Michael at six at the bar—Ann's section of the bar.

My second Wednesday with Mary was quite different. We

were just walking from breakfast when I said, " Could use some more tea." I looked around for a coffee shop. "Let's try in there."

That's the way it went all day with me—didn't get far, didn't see much, just, with Mary, drank tea here and there. A fine day it was, too; not cloudy, not raining. Yes, that's the way it went all morning and afternoon. At one point, laughing, she even said to me, "You might as well be in Dublin." Which was odd, that she said it, because that was exactly what I was wanting to say to her.

Before I went to the departure gate just now, I did say, "Have Michael bring you across. Or have him buy you a tick, and leave him at home. Hey, Michael? I'll take her over the bog, rock, moss, and heather all the way to Connemara."

"Good, Timothy, good," he says to me, afraid I'd say more. And Mary's all the while watching with serious eyes, yet smiling at us, two Irish brothers with their private language of parting.

::

Even if Michael does a thing or two in ways that I wouldn't, he's really not such a bad fellow. What Mary wanted to know, yes, he could have told her. But I suppose he was thinking that by telling her he'd either win her for good or lose her right then and there to an old idea she'd always miss. And neither way was what he wanted—that is, if he ever knows what he wants at all.

I notice when one travels how things fall off of one. Even on my way to Dublin airport two weeks ago, even before I got on the plane, little things on my mind—the extra key I'd meant to get made, the dry-cleaning I'd wanted to take in—little things like that began to fall off. And by the time the plane touched the ground in New York, for me the whole of Dublin was gone.

Then, when you're in a new place, of course new things attach, but when you leave, it happens again—now, on my way back to Dublin, bits and thoughts of New York have begun leaving me. I wonder if by the time this plane touches down, Mary, too, will be gone.

Mary—not an Irish name in this case, but it could become one. Though who knows but if after a while she'll want anything at all to do with whatever's Irish, or at least whatever's Irish with our family name.

I don't really believe in saving, but then, I just might have to keep saving it. Until I'm a husband in Ireland, a father in Ireland, a grandfather with grandchildren in Ireland. Say if they're boys like we were, I'll take them over the bog, rock, moss, and heather, over to Galway. Down to Connemara on the coast. I'll say to them as Grandfather said to us: "Me lads...."

Yes, Irish grandfathers really do speak that way, and when you're lads just over for the first time from built-up gray Dublin, you catch and remember every new thing; every word, every color of brown, blue, and green as you stand on each side of Grandfather, who puts a hand on your shoulder and looks out to the Aran Islands in Galway Bay. "Me lads, when you can see the islands...."

And if I'm going to stay in Ireland until I'm a grandfather, I'm going to speak that way, too. And I'm going to say what he said, which is what everyone there says as they look out over the bay on days when you can see the islands, that when you can see the islands it's going to rain, and when you can't see the islands, it's raining.

A LOT OF THINGS TO TELL YOU

Do I bother you?
You are kind. Very kind.
I'd like to stay here—if that pleases you.

::

Are you better? A little better?
You're making fun of me—rest a little! Rest!

::

What a pleasure to talk to you. I understand everything
you say.
    Listen to me—I'd like you to rest. I'd like you to be
happy.
    I have a lot of things to tell you. A lot of things.

::

    Most people never take the time to live—it's not difficult.
It's even very easy.
    It's so simple! Imagine!

::

How long have you been waiting for me? How long?
We'll talk about it some other time. This afternoon. This evening. Midnight. Tomorrow.

::

Everything will go all right. Everything. I'm certain of it.

::

You see? You understand me, don't you?

::

You are kind. Very. Kind.

::

I enjoy it here. I'm no longer tired. Everything is so different.

::

You look surprised. You look younger. Tell me what surprises you.

EIDETIC

Dear Hank,

I know this is unceremonious, writing on my daughter's "Care Bear" stationery but, nonetheless, you haven't written to me and I feel like our dialogue has ended abruptly. Writing to you without getting a reply is like jerking off.

Not much is happening here in Wainscott. Adrian is penis-obsessed. Fortunately next week his father is joining me so I'll let *him* deal with it. (Another reason I'm glad I'm not a single mother.)

And if you want to know what penis-obsession *means* in a four-year-old, it means him clipping little Spider-Man weapons around his penis and shooting them. And threatening his sister by holding his penis like a hose and chasing her around pretending to pee on her. (On the other hand, I did catch Emma just as she was about to tie a little doll apron and bonnet around Adrian's penis to make, "a penis woman," she told me.)

All this is too much for me. But I can relate all the way around. I mean, if *I* had a penis, I would find all *kinds* of fun things to do with it too.

Now, Hank, what is this note about what I just received from my mother? What is she talking about when she says "us"? YOU AND ME? And she says she *approves*—OF WHAT?? *RÉPONDEZ S'IL VOUS PLAÎT!*

In any case, her sensationalism knows no shame. Yesterday she called and told me in a quavering, tear-filled voice that my grandmother had fallen down the stairs. I thought it had just happened. She filled me in, blow by blow, slo-o-owly, in that teary voice with lots of sighs: how grandma landed on the concrete basement floor, that she may have been lying there for "who knows how long," that the doctors wouldn't tell the family for sure if she was ever going to walk again. Finally I asked if my grandmother was going *to die* and she responded in a perfectly normal voice that this all happened days ago and that grandma is now sitting up in her hospital bed, eating, speaking and drinking. (My mother is truly a product of the tabloid age.)

Of course, the whole thing is horrible, because even though I don't really care about most of them, I do have a vague fondness for my grandmother. Furthermore, I know a huge confrontation will happen when I don't attend either or both my grandmother's logically imminent funeral or my sister's remotely possible wedding. But what can they do? Put a familial curse on me? Cut me out of a will that I'm not in anyway?

Hank, have you ever read any interesting fiction or drama about mailmen? Not postal workers, only the people who schlep it to your door. I recently imagined a scene in which a mailman throws bunches of letters into the ocean. Can you imagine how appalled and upset certain people would be if they found out a mailman might have *done something* to their mail? There could be a public lynching. (What I'm trying to say, Hank, is, Please write.)

::

I'm going to bed now. It's very late for me (a quarter to midnight) and I've obviously missed the last letter pickup.

::

OK, now it is 5 A.M. and although I'm sipping a cup of coffee while the kids are still sleeping, I'm not *really* awake because I jumped out of bed when the alarm went off, thinking I was late or maybe reacting to a dream or something. (Ignore me if I'm babbling.)

I think that all night I dreamt about people I knew when I was in high school. I woke at 2 A.M. composing in my head the meaningful letter I would write to Shirley, my high school drug pal and sex partner who, twelve years ago, when I ran into her out in Missoula, was a telephone repair person and looked like a cowboy with breasts. Then I slept and woke again, sure that I would call and visit Ellis, my flamboyant and brilliant boyfriend but *not* sex partner (he was always gay) and show him the photo of us running naked through the campus of the college I would soon attend. I rediscovered Ellis when I taught a term in Santa Cruz and then re-rediscovered him a couple of years later on a trip (before I met you) to New York. He writes essays that often wind up in good places under different names. The last one was about his having AIDS. I'm frightened to contact him again because I think he's quite sick and even though I've never really been around one, I have a feeling I would be a lousy bedside companion for a terminally ill person.

Did I ever tell you that I have an eidetic brain? I never really thought of it as a virtue because nobody else cares if a person has this ability or not since it doesn't really translate outside one's head, but anyway I can see the wildest things clearly. I'm really at my best when I can visualize the pine floor of your house up there, and the newspaper beneath the maple table with benches at either side and something on your stove that was pretty, probably an enamel teapot.

And a beige shirt that you wore. And how I got you hard with my hair.

::

Now it's 8:30 and the kids here have had breakfast. I'm watching them through the patio door but, let's face it, you can't raise your children through glass, so this will be short.

What I wanted to tell you was my favorite passage in that insert you sent me from *Sassy* (an appallingly racy post-toddler magazine that I often did look at—and I know you did too) is the one where the foxy guy buys a "hardbound, coffee-table-size book" (and I thought Madonna's *Sex* was oversized) and then tells the cashier that she has "a good bod but no brain cells" because she short-changed him.

Who do you think are the true intellectuals? I'm a fan of both Gore Vidal and Harold Bloom although most people can't stand either of them. George Plimpton was interesting. (I wish you were here with me so you could say Yes-No-Yes or something.)

I'm seeing Adrian getting his penis out. Gotta go.

::

The mailman's not here yet, but now I have a little girl with a toothache in my lap. Poor Emmikins. I'll have her write her greetings to you—she's a very smart little girl.

::

Now it is 1 P.M. I am most definitely awake. Got your two hilarious postcards just now, along with an envelope full of annotated clippings. The cards killed me. You are so funny Hank Hillon.

But I'm trying to respond to your real letter. The older

letter about love and sex and relationships. You're right about the getting close and pulling back thing and how I did that and you too. But why when I was pregnant with Adrian? Just timing? I don't know why I did that with you. I can only make things up because I can't remember why, and my eidetic mind can't seem to see anything either. Maybe it had to do with the sex. You're right, sex can really screw things up. (You said "make you sad" but I don't feel that way although I see how you can because you are a romantic person and I'm not, although I wish I was. I'm too pragmatic.)

Sex used to define me in a sense. Especially when I was a teenager and it was one of the only ways I knew how to communicate, since I was raised in a family where sexual abuse and innuendo privileged academia and sincerity. Seduction and sex was a hard habit to break. Some time after I started college I found out that I had another way to relate to people, and after all isn't that what life is about—always looking for other people to relate to? So I changed my appearance—short hair, no makeup, and found that sexual energy towards me changed and I wasn't flirting with every dick-head on the street. Though I do tend to flirt with men and women after I know them and trust there is something about me they like that doesn't include sex. Because sexual energy between friends is inevitable especially when it's one of the biggest things you really don't know about each other. So what if I can't help but wonder about other people's sexual responses—does that make me a kind of voyeur? Anyway, I'm a *would-be* fly on the wall.

I'm glad (I hate that word).... I'm happy.... I'm pleased...? It's nice (awful).... It is *simpatico* that you now have in your life a woman who something's going on with... (no, no, no) whom you're interested in (worse). HEY DUDE, GOOD LUCK WITH THE BABE! Now for your question: How would I feel if you were married...? hmm.... I guess it would be just another thing. I had a very close friend in Santa Fe who worked at a place called The Borrowed Money Café. His name was Eugene. We tried the sex thing about ten years ago and it wasn't right, but we were (and still are in a remote sort of way) close friends. For a while, way back when neither of us had a partner. Then he met a wild Texas chanteuse, but my never-ending presence led to their demise. Years later, after I was married, he met a woman who he'd eventually marry and he said to me, "Dee," (that's what he always called me—Dee DiLorenzo), "BACK OFF!" I've always backed off but she's never been entirely comfortable with me.

And so it goes....

I'm going to stop writing this letter now.

CHICAGOO

Kim. When Kim handed me some of her husband's condoms—"Here, use these"—out of one of their bedroom dresser drawers, could she sense the astonishment I was trying my best not to show?

I did almost try to ask Kim a practical question, but I stopped myself, imagining her answering it sternly, or, more likely, in exasperation: "Jimmy. *Who counts condoms?*"

::

Estelle. The last time I saw Estelle was at the movie theater where we'd arranged to meet. "Make sure it's a short one, Jimmy—no epics," she'd said over the phone while I checked the newspaper listings. We were on the sidewalk in line for tickets when her husband walked by. He didn't say a word to either of us, but we weren't breaking any rules that I knew of.

The only rule I did know of was, yes, Estelle and I could spend time together and talk and drink tea or whatever like that we did—and, really, that was all I preferred to do—as long as he didn't have to witness it. That is, in their house which he had helped pay for. After all, who was I but some ex-boyfriend from twenty years previous? Until I moved back to the area, she'd never even mentioned me.

For the better part of the first year, I'd deliberately

avoided her. When we finally did meet up, I told her so. She didn't ask why, but just gave me an inscrutable look and started talking about something else altogether.

After many meetings, and though I'd sworn to myself I never would, one time I asked, "Estelle, what about the guy on the island?"

"What guy? What island?"

Back when I first knew her, although I spent many occasional nights in Estelle's bed, I always left her the virgin I found her. What was she then, seventeen? Or eighteen? That's not so very young, but I was looking at it differently: she was just out of high school and I was already through university. Plenty of time.

Then she ran away with some guy who lived on an island. She came back to me after a week of that, but I wasn't having any of it. Which didn't make any sense even to me at the time, because I obviously cared for her, and I missed her a lot.

::

If Estelle didn't know what I was talking about, that meant she didn't remember her first time. I frequently recalled mine, a few years before I met Estelle, because it was in a house near where I live now and pass every day.

She—I sometimes see her around—had said it was her first time, too. But I read long after in a magazine poll that twenty-five percent of girls say it is when it is, twenty-five percent say it is when it isn't, twenty-five percent say it isn't when it isn't, and twenty-five percent say it isn't when it is.

::

"I like to run fast, Jimmy." Kim has said to me more than once. "I can't seem to do anything else fast, so I run fast."

There's no flies on Kim, though; nothing dragged-out about her. What she means is that having her kids and husband and everything else that goes with them for much of every day keeps her from doing all she'd like to do, and with the speed she'd prefer. Not that she'd want to give up anything she has, but Kim does enjoy extending herself back into her sometimes-imploding world with things like running fast. When we first met, Kim looked me up and down and then said, "Do you swim, Jimmy? I think you'd make a good swimmer."

::

Within days of starting our affair, Kim, quite matter-of-factly, told me she'd told a friend of hers all about us. When I heard that, I nearly jumped out of my skin, for while I didn't exactly know this friend, I knew I moved in the same circles she did.

"*What* did you tell her?"

"You know, my friend won't repeat this stuff."

"But *what?*"

"That you had exquisite lips—then I told her everything. How it was my idea, how I set it up, the time, the place. How you resisted...."

For a moment I just looked at her. It wasn't my first, or even second relationship with a married woman, but it was the first time I knew of that it had fallen from the realm of the hidden.

"Look," she said, "I don't know what you're thinking, but you know, everyone has secrets."

"*I* don't," I said, as if it were a sure thing. If I was trying to caution or intimidate her, it didn't work.

"Jim-eee!" she squealed, laughing. Kim already seemed to know me well enough to be sure that if I stopped and thought it over and started counting, I'd find out I had dozens or hundreds or even millions of them.

::

Holly. When it came to married women, Holly was the first. It happened in my car, after I'd offered to drive her home from work. I was shocked, really. Even in subsequent, similar situations, I always was, each and every first time. Not so much because of any specific actions, but by some general, insistent needs I'd find there, ones I'd incorrectly figured must be being met. Wherever they come from, you'd think I'd get used to such things, but I've never been able to.

As for single women, I suppose less furtiveness means less shock. Besides, at such times, often I was the desiring one. And when it comes to the times I myself was married or such, they've all turned out to be difficult situations for me to confront today—it's hard to believe that where there once was, had to be, such familiarity, now there's almost none. But that's the way it remains.

::

Holly I met when she had only one child, the first boy. She and I have sought each other out since, yet my main memory of her goes back to that first child. I was sitting on a rock wall one autumn day when they came toward me, she with her yellow hair, he with his red. The same colors as the fallen leaves they were walking through.

Whenever no one was around, Holly and I would hold hands, lightly. That day, she and her little boy were. With them it looked like the process of a near-perfect birth: incomplete, and through her fingertips.

::

The kid used to tell me some good jokes. "What happens if Chicago gets too hot and starts to melt?"
"What?"
"Chicagoo."

::

People call it cheating. I don't know. Once in a while I've successfully resisted, wanting to keep the friendship, I would be thinking, pure and open to the sunlight. Probably always a mistake?

Sometimes they'd ask me to do things their husbands wouldn't do. Or do things they would never ask their husbands to do. Or do things that their husbands asked them to do, but they wouldn't do with their husbands.

::

As for Estelle, who's kind of a special case as I knew her, then didn't, and now do again, after the thing at the movies, I didn't see her or hear from her for one month, then two. I began to feel there were new rules—no phone calls or anything to or from me. And that perhaps she'd begun to agree that these new rules were good ones. Somehow I decided to write her a letter and send it in care of her mother in the suburbs. I didn't say much in it. I did close by asking how her mother was.

Not right away, but soon I got a letter in return: Hi Jimmy, she'd been busy, the kids and school this, the house and yard that, she'd bump into me soon, oh her mother was fine and—Estelle's not coy or stupid—didn't I think it odd, us writing letters like this when we lived in the same city within walking distance of each other?

TANGENITAL

Dear Yvonne,

I would like to introduce myself. My name is Bradley Paul O'Donnel and I am from Spring Creek, Indiana. You probably have no idea where that is, but "The Creek" is in a small suburb of the more well-known city of Muncie.

I am 22 years old and am currently studying science and pre-law at the University of Florida in Gainesville. I decided to write to you because I am a huge fan of yours and, well, another year is almost past, and I thought it would be nice to take the time to let you know how much some of your fans appreciate you—you definitely top *my* list of favorite celebrities.

I am sure you get plenty of fan mail, and with your busy modeling schedule the chances of you reading this are slim to none, but still I wanted to try to let you know that I always look forward to your appearances.

I am not sure how else to express my sincere admiration for you. I can't fathom what it must be like to have thousands of people placing me on a pedestal like they do you, but the thing is you still seem very down to earth. That's the quality I admire most about you.

I don't personally know any models—let alone any *supermodels*—at this point in my life but some years back my father, who was working for the Woolite Corporation, was in charge of hiring models for them. They were not, of course, at your level, and they certainly, there, weren't ever wearing teeny bikinis, but some of them were, I think, quite attractive.

I remember two of those models especially (this was before I was, I guess, even 12 years old). One was Karen and one was Heidi. They were both (unlike you) brunettes, and they each had white, white skin. At the time, of course, I was just as interested in the chocolate cake and stuff my mother would make and leave for them. Still, I often wonder where they are today, what they are doing—I mean, did they ever "make it" as full-fledged models?

When I am not attending university here I scoot home to my parents' place for a few days. When I told my father I was going to do up a letter to "the model on the wall," (I put up a picture of you in my room there) he didn't think it was too crazy an idea, but he did advise me not to write anything cheesy.

Yvonne, I know you are a stunningly beautiful woman who must get a lot of e-mails and letters, so how can I hope to convince you that you should pay attention to mine?

First, I am *not* an autograph collector, and I don't have any trouble getting girlfriends, even great-looking ones (for sure there are a lot on the beaches down here). But from what I've read and heard about you, I just think it's a mistake for you not to know me personally.

If you wrote me back, you wouldn't have to sign your letter, so there's no autograph angle. If you called me, e-mailed me, same thing. I just want the chance to be able to persuade you that I stand apart from any other fans of yours.

Yvonne, I have this theory. I call it *tangenitality*. It's like this: If I go to bed with a woman ("A") who has been to bed with another man who has been to bed with another woman ("B"), then, while I certainly have a genital relationship with "A", I also have what I've come to call a *tangenital* (tangentially genital) connection to "B".

I haven't thought my theory out completely yet, but I know I'm just not ever very happy with any of the women I'm around, and if you could think of someone in the Gainesville area—or, probably less likely, even around Muncie (I'll be there over the holidays)—who you think could provide me with this kind of connection to you, then, well, I'd be, maybe for the first time ever, *really satisfied.*

Please think this over and write me, call me, whatever. If for some reason you are not able to fill my request, I will understand fully, and you would still be one of my favorite public figures and human beings. In the meantime I do look forward to hearing from you and am happy in knowing that you know how much I appreciate your work.

Stay beautiful inside and out—I wish you luck, love and laughter always, Yvonne. Merry Christmas! Have a Happy!

Your fan for life,

Brad

ME. YOU. LOVE.

My wife, Ellen, spends $300 a month on her face. Her gym costs $180, Pilates $300, personal trainer $300.

> ***UPSTAIRS—Phase 1 (Fall):***
> *Demolish tub, sink, shelving & shower.*
> *Build one dormer window.*

We rent. $5000. She pays half. But we own a small house near New London, fixing it up. Fifteen minutes past there, almost three hours from here.

> *Build new shower with tiles.*
> *Install freestanding sink & water-efficient toilet.*
> *Redesign & build shelves/cabinets for towels*
> *& bathroom supplies.*

On average, $1000 a month for Ellen's clothes. Hair, another $400. I pay the phones, but she pays utilities, about $150.

> ***UPSTAIRS—Front Bedroom (facing lake):***
> *Demolish skylight. Build two dormer windows to*
> *replace it.*

I know Ellen used to spend $500 on her face. She does say that now she tries to keep $200 back for *emergencies*, but I'm never sure if that's really the same $200 she might not now be spending on her face—"How do I look, David?"

"Great! OK!" Really, she does. Everywhere. Always. Manicures? Pedicures? What—say, $35 two or three times a month?

UPSTAIRS—Back Bedroom (facing garage):
Demolish north skylight. Build two dormer
windows to replace it. Replace south skylight with
new skylight.

Eating, in and out, about $1700, at least, for both of us —we split it. Over a year, travel works out to $500 a month each, local transportation another $250 each. Entertainment, tips, say a thousand a month—more or less we split that too.

"David! I'm starved!" That's Ellen coming back now.

"We'll order in," I say. "I'll take care of it." She's too hungry to argue. She agrees.

New roof. New, better quality shingles.

Married three years now. No kids. Not yet.

DOWNSTAIRS—Phase 2 (Spring):
Expand Kitchen.
Demolish existing kitchen.
Extend kitchen out into yard—square footage to
be determined (accommodating 50-foot setback
into design & back toward garage, to the depth
of the existing washing machine closet.)
Concrete footing under new kitchen extension.
New glass door out to porch toward lake.
Wall of windows facing lake and wrapping
around side yard to wall.
Install kitchen cabinets, stove, refrigerator in
"L" formation.
One or two windows overlooking back deck
(depending on cabinets.)

A story was told to me once, a true story. I could point out to anyone where the whole thing culminated, just as it was pointed out to me. A nice guy, good-looking, good job, good background, good prospects, and no problem with women—he always could have, and had, his pick. Until one day he notices a woman in his neighborhood, and, first look, her face fixes in his brain, I guess, and all other women become, pretty soon, unsatisfying. He withdrew, like a monk—*almost* like a monk.

On one hand, he must have been saving himself, everything in himself for this woman, until, whenever, he saw her again. But, one night, he can't stand it, being alone, the mental tension, maybe, and the physical. So he goes—he had no need to, I understand, at any other time in his life—he goes to, I don't think it was an inexpensive establishment, some kind of house of prostitution. He's shown women to choose from—and there she is!

Did he choose her? That's what I asked. Yes. And then I asked, Does he marry her? No, no, no, he does not marry her.

> *Revisit plumbing.*
> *Make sure all plumbing is up to date.*
> *New water heater.*
> *New water filtration system.*
> *Possibly new toilet in downstairs bathroom.*
> *Try to increase pressure in upstairs bathroom.*

Anything else? Well, Ellen has medical and dental coverage, but there's probably a couple of hundred dollars outside of that. And New York—probably anywhere, really—can vacuum the money, if you've got it, out of your pocket as you just walk down the street, so, in a month, $300? $400? Oh—and she gets a maid in one day a week, $65 each time.

In my own case, before Ellen, of course there was someone else. She—well, she was someone who I felt as if I'd always known and always would. And I think she felt the same about me.

I want to think that, wherever she is now, she under-stands why we couldn't go on like we were, that no good would come of it, almost nothing happening, hardly any-thing getting done day after day together, just each of us thinking the same thing: Me. You. Love. So I left.

There's the bell. "Ellen! Food's here!"

SCAR

Patty told me that when Cal got sent over to France, where his company's head office is, for six months, right away he sent her back a bunch of European chocolate bars. "How did they *taste?*" she answered him over the phone. "I was missing you so much I ate them like a wolf and got my period an hour later. That means *I* didn't eat them, Cal, my hormones did. So I'm not sure if they tasted good."

Since Patty got the lumpectomy, she won't sleep with anyone but Cal, because he was the one who went with her to the hospital and wasn't surprised when he saw the scar.

Cal gets back for good in October; their wedding's in November. "This will be a marriage that makes *sense,*" she's always telling me, her buddy, Suzanne—I'm long divorced. It's hard for each of us to believe it's going to be her first marriage, considering that she hasn't ever spent much time by herself.

"Twenty-four hours, Suzanne. I wasn't even sixteen when that's what I was feeling I wanted to do, spend twenty-four hours with a boy. I wasn't thinking *all* of it in bed, but that's pretty much the way it usually turned out. Even back then I couldn't stand to be *alone,* Suzanne. I'm sorry, but for all the time up to Cal I was, I *was* easy. Now *you're* easy, Suzanne. *Relatively.*"

Twenty-four, forty-eight, seventy-two hours. Bedroom, bathroom, sometimes the kitchen, and back to the bedroom. "It's a *power feeling,* Suzanne." Then in the first apartment she got herself, she bought a waterbed, a heated one. "But even with these itty bitty moves of mine, sometimes I'd start to sweat so bad, Suzanne, I'd have to turn the sucker off."

::

For a long time now, Patty's had it figured out she can't have kids. Something to do with the last of those five abortions. Up to the third, she was still living at home, sharing a room with her little sister who—Patty finally had to explain it all to her—didn't even know what an abortion *was.*

"If I couldn't have my own kids, I always had other people's, didn't I, Suzanne?" She means my three, all taller than Patty now. "Rhonda I remember when she was just a tiny girl. Tommy was a baby in diapers. And Kelly, the little jigger—I said to her, 'See you round like a doughnut,'—what was she, five? And she says back *instantly,* 'Like a cup of coffee. Like a pizza. Like a bagel....' *Smoke gets in your eyes,* Suzanne. I'll be forty-one years old and crying at my own wedding."

::

It was after about only thirty-six hours with Cal, when she was in the shower, that she felt the lump. He *was* divorcing at the time. The operation was three weeks later. That's when she started thinking that finally getting married would make perfect sense.

"Su falls in love, Patty doesn't fall in love. For how long have we known each other—really sixteen years? *Good* girl, you. I was always *bad,* Suzanne."

The wedding reception will be small, in the city, at my place. "On a *Sunday,*" Patty had insisted. A dry reception afterward—fruit drinks and soda only. "I was drunk last Sunday night. *I can't believe people drink on a Sunday night.*" She kept saying it to everyone at the bar. "*I sleep a week for every night I drink.*" Everybody kept buying and she kept drinking. "*I am not going to make it to work tomorrow."* Everybody at the bar was killing themselves laughing and she never said out loud anything about Cal who wouldn't be back for months or the wide, raised purplish line on her blue-white breast that was never, ever going to go away.

::

"People look different right up close, don't they, Suzanne?" Patty had seen Cal several times from a distance and hadn't thought much of him. But when he took her for a walk one night after the bar closed, she kept falling into him and looking up at his face. "I wanted to go home and write him a letter to tell him what he looked like up close, Suzanne."

Cal has a weekend place, an old house out in the country. Once, he left Patty there alone overnight and when he got back the next afternoon he found her blacked out from drinking almost a whole fifth of whiskey straight from the bottle. She had on his flannelette pajamas, her hair was standing on end, she was on the floor propped up by pillows and the TV was up as high as the remote would take it. Cal got so angry he grabbed all her clothes and threw them out over the front yard. "And then I was a hangover case—it must have taken me fifteen minutes to pick my blue wool sweater out of the thorny bushes the next day, Suzanne. I'd *take* the twelve-step program, I would, if it wasn't for the Jesus thing."

::

It's a marriage that makes sense to Patty and she has it all planned. After the ceremony and the reception, it'll be just like any other trip to Cal's old house in the country, except for the plastic carnations decorating the car. She'll say *she* wants to drive, and then kick off her shoes. "You can't drive in high heels, Suzanne, you start jerking the car. But in some places it's illegal to drive in bare feet!"

Before starting the engine, Patty always looks at herself in the rear-view mirror. Will her wedding day have been a bad-hair one? Will her lipstick be still on just her lips?

It's only about an hour's drive to get out there, but about half-way she always has to pee. "So bad I can taste it—I don't know why, Suzanne. Even if I go before we start. It's like my kidneys know where they're going and are thrilled by the trip."

So Patty will pull over to the side of the road. When she gets out and goes to squat behind the car, Cal will slide over into the driver's seat. "That's my baby," or something like that, she'll say to him as she climbs back in.

Patty knows a lot of what's going to happen when they get there: they'll pull the car up close to the house, and Cal will carry her up the two steps to the porch and then over the threshold.

"I'll phone you right away, Suzanne, I promise. I wonder how I'll *feel*. I wonder what I'll *say*." Last summer when she phoned me from there for the very first time, she said it was way, way out in the middle of nowhere and no one could smell it or hear it or see you—"The *barbecue*, Suzanne!"— she meant there were no neighbors for the smoke to bother, you could cook outside with the music up loud all night long and even go around without a shirt on, though she would never do that.

HELEN SAYS

Laura's masking.

That's what Helen says—Helen in the other of the bedrooms of their two-bedroom—"Laura's masking."

And those looks of Laura's, so many in that face—is each of them a mask?

"I don't think of it that way," says Helen. "And even if one is, and whether it's a mask that comes from masking, or a mask that hides the masking—I don't think of it that way," says Helen. "I just think now that that's just Laura. And no matter what look is on her face, she's masking."

Masking. Helen says not to think of it as covering or disguising or concealing. Helen says to understand it is not to take it as something put up front and over like a mask. Helen says it's not like that.

"Think of a glove," says Helen. "One that dulls your sense of touch, but as if it were worn *underneath* the surface of your hand. Or a sound inside you that you carry to dampen outside sound. Or a filter that tones down what you see, not like sunglasses—*behind* your eyes. That's masking," Helen says. "That's the way it is with Laura. And Laura's always masking."

Always?

Helen says Laura's good at it, has had lots of practice, that it comes without thinking now.

But always?

Helen says that maybe if you get Laura laughing really hard, or if you find Laura crying, or if you catch Laura just waking up or just about to fall asleep, then maybe she's not masking. "Of course, there's dreaming—not that I know what Laura dreams," says Helen. "But while she's dreaming, I don't think she could still keep masking."

"You've known Laura a long time."

"A long time."

"Before you and Laura took this apartment together, when she was married, was she also masking then?"

"When she was married and before—before she even thought of getting married."

"So you must know Laura well. Do you think she *knows* she's masking?"

"Maybe she didn't know exactly at first, but by now she must know. Of course she wouldn't admit it, not to herself or anyone else—that's part of masking."

"You ever try to talk to her about it?"

"She doesn't want to. That's another part of masking."

"You two talk to each other a lot about other things?"

"We don't really have that much to say to each other anymore."

"So Laura doesn't tell you everything...."

"Someone who's masking and who doesn't want to talk about it might not have that much else to tell."

"Wasn't she seeing someone a while back?"

"Jim. A nice guy, Jim," says Helen. "But, to Laura, Jim could have been almost anybody. And she must have known that. And that's part of the reason why she was masking then. Why she is masking now. Why she's always masking."

Why? Why is Laura masking?

"Because she thinks she shouldn't have to mask," says Helen.

Says Helen. And how does Helen know?

"Oh," says Helen. "I know masking."

Helen doesn't catch herself and say that she has masked. Or even that she masks but of course is not now masking. No. All Helen says in the other bedroom of their two-bedroom is, "I know masking."

SNOWSUIT

He had on his snowsuit. He wasn't even cold.

"Are you all right?"

The first time the lady said it, he didn't know what she was saying.

"What?" He sat up.

"Are you all right?"

"I'm all right."

"I've been standing across the street for fifteen minutes. I was walking by and saw you weren't moving. So I watched —you didn't move at all."

Well, what's so wrong with—but he just looked at her and said, "I was all right."

"You'll catch cold, just lying in the snow like that."

He wouldn't. "This snowsuit's really warm."

"How old are you? Nine?"

"Eight. Almost nine."

"Aren't you getting a little big for snowsuits?"

What else did she ask him? Was he sleeping? "I wasn't sleeping." Just looking at the clouds? "There's no clouds." At the sky, then?

Is that what he was doing?

"Nothing to do? You should be busy doing something," she said. "Playing with your friends. Just looking at the sky like that, you must get bored."

He was all right. He wasn't cold. He wasn't sleeping. He

wasn't looking. He wasn't doing anything, so maybe he
didn't look busy. He doesn't know if he was busy or not, but
he wasn't bored.

::

He's sorry he worried the lady. He didn't know it was
fifteen minutes. He didn't know anyone would watch him.
Maybe he should have been in the back yard. But where he
was when he started lying there was in the front yard.
Maybe he just started thinking. But he's not sure what he
was thinking. Fifteen minutes? He wasn't cold. He wasn't
bored.

::

People get ideas about you. When he told his big sister
about the lady, she said the older you get, the more people
get ideas about you.
"Because you get taller?"
Older, his sister meant. The *older* you get, the more people
get ideas about you.
"I don't want people to get ideas about me."
His sister said it didn't matter, they're going to.

::

He's sorry he made the lady worry. He's sorry she had to
stop and watch him for fifteen minutes. He didn't move for
fifteen minutes, she said—but sometimes you forget just
what you're doing and where you are. In the front yard, or in
the back yard, or in your room. In his room, if anyone saw
him now, they'd think he was just looking at the ceiling. But
that's not really what he's doing. He doesn't look busy. His
eyes are open. He might be thinking, but he doesn't always

remember what he was thinking. He doesn't look busy, but maybe he is. He's not bored.

::

He's going to ask his sister how to make sure people get the right ideas about you. Because people do get ideas about you. Maybe it's fine if somebody gets the right ideas about you.

::

He had on his snowsuit. His snowsuit's really warm.

He wants to be busy, but he doesn't want to be just busy. He doesn't want to be just busy, and he doesn't want to be bored.

FREDERICK

1. "Never the same hotel twice, Marie." I understood him perfectly. And there's so many hotels in this big old world.

2. *Good* hotels. Good sheets. Everything just right, the whole bit!

3. "Do you like *this*, Marie?" "And *this*, Marie?" "*This* way— or *this* way, Marie?" My God, my God, my God.

4. O.K., so we're in separate hotels tonight, in different cities. It can happen. In the meantime, *the next time*.

5. I picked up a book in the lobby newsstand, *The Cat Who Saw Stars*. I was hoping it was a kind of children's book for adults—but it was a mystery! So I went back down and bought a *stack* of magazines.

6. We didn't talk long on the phone. What was there to say? My presence. His absence. Nothing to do but wait. For weeks? Anyway, for our next chance.

7. Television on—but no sound!

8. I could call his airline to check if everything he said is true—I did that once. But we *burn* for each other, why wouldn't it always be true?

9. He always grabs me somewhere *after* he says his good-byes—I *love* it!

10. God, I hate when one of us has to leave in the morning —and never together.

11. If he and I could be, were together all the time, would it be like this, could it stay like this?

12. *Frederick*. Not *Fred*. Never *Freddie*. *Frederick*. (He's not even here and he has my full attention.)

13. I feel cold now and I'm not sure how to get warm. If I could just get angry at him, maybe that would heat my body up.

14. There's a way he pays attention to my mouth, my lower lip, that makes *me* swell, I swear.

15. Code Names: He calls me ——————, I call him ——————. (He knows I keep a journal, he said I must *never* write those names down.)

16. Such a common fantasy. Her away, even for the day. *Me* in their bed. In the middle of the afternoon. Lots of light. An ordinary, logical, common fantasy—but not one bit boring!

17. The e-mail thing, the text-messaging thing, the cell-phone thing. Then the hotel thing. All over America. (*But*— I have to wait.)

18. Missed connections, like tonight. And now I resist touching myself, alone.

19. We always have to hurry. It doesn't sound ideal, I know. Not having to hurry, now that *sounds* like it would be perfect, but hurrying, having to, can also be delicious.

20. It started like this: just him saying, *Nice to meet you, Marie*, and me, while I just said his own name back to him, at the

same time thinking, *I want you to take me to a hotel room someday, Frederick. I think I'll like the way you'd make me feel.*

21. Almost bedtime. It's going to be a rainy day tomorrow. (I like the sound of that word, *bedtime*.)

22. In Denver once, we had room service before *and* after. The lemon pie was really good.

23. Did I have a feeling he wouldn't show up tonight? Maybe, but I always have that feeling. And then—almost always—he shows up!

24. One night, in the middle of it, I told him, *I wish you were my brother*, and then I thought whatever will he think? But he didn't miss a beat, he said, *I wish you were my sister.* And we got hardly any sleep that night!

25. On nights like tonight I can start to worry that Frederick is hiding from me because he knows what I might want. More than one night?

26. *God* I'm glad I met Frederick.

27. I hope I have good dreams tonight.

28. I hope tomorrow will be a nice day for me.

29. I want to go to sleep, but I don't want to stop thinking about him.

30. I think I'll lie down and close my eyes.

31. I don't want to just wake up—I want him to wake me up.

32. He was doing me spoon-style when I turned my head to ask him—I almost *never* mention her—if he does it this way with his wife. I whispered it, really, but he had to have heard

me. He not only didn't answer, there was nothing about him that showed any reaction to what I'd asked.

33. She can't watch him every minute. She must know that. She doesn't know about us, but *still*.

34. I couldn't take it. I mean, O.K., let's say he was mine, with me. Probably she'd get the house. And then me, one day, alone, just for an hour or two, and I'd start thinking he's back in that house that was his, stealing a few minutes with her.

35. I'm not much younger than her. She'd think it was because I am, even by just four years. She'd be a little bit right in that sometimes that's all there is to it, but sometimes it's *more* than that.

36. Anyway, she'd hate me. I don't hate her. Hardly ever think of her.

37. I'll get some sleep now. Get up early, take a shower, dry my hair. Have breakfast at the airport.

38. Good night, my love, my lover. (Sometimes it's enough. Sometimes it's not enough. Sometimes it's enough. Sometimes it's not enough.)

39. I feel sick.

40. Sometimes it's not enough.

41. Good night, my love, my lover.

THINGS WE SAY TO COPS (THINGS COPS SAY TO US)

This and the following piece were written for Thomas Beller of "Mr. Beller's Neighborhood" in response to his perpetual imperative "Tell Mr. Beller a story" about the author's existence in New York City.

1971. When I was still a student and first visited New York City, the couple at whose place I was staying suggested we take a walk to the piers near the entrance to the Holland Tunnel. While we were crossing the roadway there, where the signs clearly prohibit pedestrians from crossing, a policemen who saw us yelled, "Get out of there, you fucks!"

1978. Soon after moving to New York, I parked my car, with its still-out-of-state plates, in Times Square (in what was clearly a no-standing zone) because a couple of visiting friends wanted to get out and look around. I was leaning on the car door when a policeman on horseback came riding by. While I did my best to appear an innocent tourist, he looked at my plates, then at me and said, "Move it, you fuck."

1987. Recently, I told a teenager who was smoking a cigarette in an elevator that he should put it out. "You a cop?" he asked.

1981. When, in a supermarket checkout line, I suggested to a fellow who had butted in front of the woman ahead of me that he move to the back, the woman turned around and said, "So, you're a cop?"

1983. Shopping with a friend at a used-clothing store, I found, among the $180 "Genuine Swedish Army Issue" long, lined, black leather coats, a similar NYPD coat for $80.

It was in perfect shape and it fit just right. I sought out a salesperson and asked, "Why is it so much cheaper?"

"Nobody knows from Swedish army officers," said the clerk, "but a cop coat…"

Undeterred, I asked the person I was with, "Should I get it?"

"Are you crazy?" she said. "It makes you look like a cop."

Shortly thereafter, a man I know found himself walking beside what he described as a beautiful young woman in midtown one day. He said he couldn't help being confused by her appearance. She was wearing rather delicate shoes, an expensive watch, a finely tailored skirt and blouse, and good jewelry and was carrying a partially wrapped single long-stemmed red rose—all right so far, but she also had on what looked like an old, short leather police jacket. My friend became even more confused when she kept looking his way and smiling.

"I felt like Gee, I should respond," he told me, "but instead I crossed the street."

"You thought she was a cop, right?" I guessed.

"No," he went on, "It wouldn't bother me so much if she was a cop. I was thinking, What if she's also the friend of a cop?"

1980. Driving in Manhattan one day with a fellow I work with, I stopped at a light alongside a two-man patrol car.

"Pigs!" my co-worker, a veteran of Berkeley student-radical days, blurted out, loudly enough that I was thankful that both of their car windows and ours were closed. I told him that I'd read that these days young Lower East Side felons refer to the police merely as "pests."

"Well," he sneered, "what do you call them?"

1982. A neighbor of mine who makes large, colorful masks figured that the pre-Halloween weekend would be a fitting time to sell his product, and that the sidewalks of SoHo, with its upscale crowds, would be the perfect place. But he had no license, and the police caught him and confiscated his masks. As his wares were being loaded into a police truck an officer told him that besides having to appear in court and face a probable $100 fine, he'd have to come down to the station and pay $65 to get his masks back.

"Sixty-five dollars!" exclaimed my neighbor. "A guy I know only had to pay $20! Why is it $65 for me?"

The cop could have explained that the retrieval fee was $65 when the vendor sells in an area where selling is prohibited, as my neighbor had done, whereas if the vendor is merely selling without a license, the fee is $20.
But the cop didn't.

"Because," he said instead, looking at him, then over at the masks, "because I don't like your faces."

THE BOWERY SCENE

1. Recently, a cousin of mine stopped over on his way from Beirut, a city which now has most of its politics in the street, but almost no sanitation services. Standing outside my door, he looked down the Bowery and marveled, "They keep it so clean!"

2. My most persistent fantasy is that one day, when I'm gathering up the garbage that the bums have sifted through and scattered on the sidewalk out front, along comes Harry Reasoner. I'm dressed for being with garbage and the story he's doing on the Bowery. He says to me, "How'd you like a square meal and a cup of coffee? You don't mind the cameras, do you?

3. When the real estate agent sent me to look at the place where I now live, on the Bowery, I almost didn't go. To walk down here is not so much to take your life in your hands, but your change purse. A half-dozen panhandlers at 25 cents, that's...

4. A woman I know who moved from the United States to England was showing me around her neighborhood in London when we came upon a shabby-looking man collapsed on the sidewalk. She ran inside her house and got a blanket for him. After the ambulance she called had departed, she remarked to me, "In New York I used to just step over them."

5. Motorists waiting in traffic on the Bowery are faced with a brigade of bums who are going to wipe their windshields, like it or not, need it or not. Some refuse to pay for the service, while others give change, or bills, or a handy gift. Still others, squirming I disgust, learn that the bums and themselves are participants in the same society and that no matter how much you pay for a car or how shiny you keep it, a drooling man with dirty cloth can revoke these privileges, if just for a little while, on the Bowery.

6. Last spring, I was wakened by the amplified words "Back on the sidewalk!" I heard it a few times but could not give it meaning. The next day things were different on the Bowery. Police on loudspeakers were ordering bums working the stopped cars for change to get "back on the sidewalk." That evening, one who did not get of the street fast enough was cornered by two policemen who poked around until they found his wine bottle which, with a nightstick, one cracked in his pocket.

7. A bum can be a beacon. Once, outside a fashionable shop on 59th Street, I saw an old hobo spot a half-eaten candy bar still in its wrapper, on the sidewalk. As he contemplated it, some passersby pointed callously, some laughed nervously, some smiled sympathetically, and some acquired what I took to be thoughtful, almost introspective expressions. Nobody ignored him. He was a beacon.

8. Not all bums drink. Not all smoke. Not all ask for money and some will not take it if it is offered.

9. It's no fun being a bum. There are the campfires, but it's not romantic to be cold, hungry, homeless unless you have hope of warmth, food, shelter.

10. It is easy to look out on the Bowery and say, "There are the bums." Encountering one, however, even one who asks to "bum a quarter" or tells you he's "on the bum" the word "bum" slips away in one's mind, perhaps given over to a "man" of "fellow," or probably, no label at all.

11. Last winter, the city, having a surplus of homeless men, charter-bused them nightly up to a dormitory on Ward's island, and, in the mornings, gave them subway tokens to get back to the Bowery.

12. Free thanksgiving diners at a couple of the missions draw hundreds of homeless men and women who usually frequent other areas of Manhattan. The milling and mixing of these people with needy tenement dwellers and Bowery regulars combine with the classic quiet of Thanksgiving Day to give the area the atmosphere of a religious festival. Some of these pilgrims linger for days, feeling at home on the Bowery.

13. One morning, a platoon of sanitation men descended on the Bowery cleaning up all the wine bottles. That afternoon a U.N. motorcade took the Bowery route to take the Chinese delegation to Chinatown.

14. Some real-estate developers, some co-op owners, some shops that attract mainly suburban customers want to clean up the Bowery, sanitize it, make it safe for money. They can try. Meanwhile, men with plenty of time to pass will pass it with Night Train wine. Incoherent babblers will be released from psychiatric institutions into the cool fats world. Amputees will sling their extras clothes over a crutch. And they'll all find their way to the Bowery.

15. Do I feel at home on the Bowery? A few years ago, I forgot to finish addressing a letter to a friend of mine, a col-

lege student. It was mailed with only his name and "University of Toronto" on the envelope. He got it. He wrote back to me that someone once wrote to "Albert Einstein, Europe." He got it. Recently, my mother, who lives in another country, wrote to "Rick Rofihe, Bowery, New York." Do I feel at home? I got it.

NORTHEAST OF EDEN:
11 TALES OF SERPENTS
(WHAT'S IN THE GRASS ISN'T SPLENDOR)

1. I don't know very much about snakes, just that I grew up far enough north in North America that there were no venomous or constricting snakes around, and that if you saw a snake there was no good reason to be afraid. Still, it can't be denied that to most people, snakes are startling—you see a stick but then you see it's a snake. It was startling in the Bible and it's startling on your lawn.

2. In the country, when my cat killed a bird, I told no one. When he killed a snake, I told everyone; no one ever said I should put a bell on him because he kills snakes.

3. New York City is a scary place. One begins to sense this when taking note of the many pet shops selling 90-cent mice, the preferred live food of pet boa constrictors kept by many New Yorkers. "There's hardly a block without a boa," said one mouse dealer. "It's scary."

4. G. Gordon Liddy, of Watergate fame, said in his book Will that he didn't want to be afraid of anything so as to be able to act freely in all situations. However, he was afraid of rats and decided to overcome his fear by roasting and eating a rat. This, like many of Mr. Liddy's actions, though amusing, and

all right for Mr. Liddy, holds little promise for the common, fearful man. After all, won't anyone who is afraid of say, snakes, probably be afraid to eat one, even a poached one with sauce? Also, do we overcome our fears, or our enemies, by consuming them or their kind? Soviet leader Nikita Khrushchev didn't say, "We will ingest you." Further, even if you ate one snake, it doesn't mean you wouldn't be afraid of the next one you saw (or were served).

5. A while back, a small-city newspaper in the Northeast dropped the Doonesbury comic strip over its use of the term "knocked up". The editors published a lot of letters concerning the matter—one, written by a person who was either a master of irony or really afraid of snakes, was headlined "Afraid of Snakes" and went like this: "Sirs: Yes, sure, keep Doonesbury going. If I want to read it or not it's still OK. I have been reading your newspaper since 1929. I am really scared of snakes. If I see a picture of a snake in any newspaper, I soon burn the paper or throw it out of my house. If I see a snake on TV, I shut it off. Lizards, etc., are OK. If I see a snake two inches long, he takes his road and I take mine."

6. My brother, a clothier, tells of a businessman he knew who imported goose down from the Far East to use in the manufacture of ski jackets. The fellow was wearing one of his own products one day when it began to feel askew. He tugged at it—but it tugged right back. He whipped off the jacket, flinging it on the ground—a snake egg had been imported with the down, and had hatched. (When my brother tells this story, he always gets asked: "What kind of snake?" "Did he kill it?" "Did he feel like a father?" "Did the guy make sleeping bags, too?")

7. Snakes have no eyelids, no hips, no lobby in Washington (some creatures do!) and little support at home.

8. One summer I heard of a rural woman who became distraught upon discovering snakes in her basement. Believing that these snakes were punishment for past sins, she thought to get rid of them by confessing her life's wrongdoings, for absolution, to anyone who'd listen. Different people told me a few things she'd divulged, always sins like "I was unreasonable with my daughter when she was growing up," or "I was impatient with my in-laws,"—the forgiveness of which just might not drive out snakes, or even reseal a good-sized can of worms.

9. If you have a psychiatrist and you dream of snakes, don't tell him/her about it. The symbolism may give you more things to fear.

10. Not too long ago I came upon an unfamiliar term, "land eel", in a magazine article. I consulted an old fellow, a fisherman, about it. "Land eels?" He gave me a look usually reserved for tourists. "Eels is eels, they all got gills. If they have to travel over land sometimes, they're still plain eels." When I asked him why anyone would use such a term, he said: "Probably meant snakes. Some people scared t'see a snake. Some might be scared to write one down."

11. I was talking to a naturalist from Pittsburgh about snakes and she said there were some dangerous ones in Pennsylvania's Allegheny Mountains. "Pennsylvania?" I worried. "That's close. I live in New York State. Are there any poisonous snakes in New York State?" Her facial muscles shifted and she took a quick long trip—two seconds to another time and place; two seconds back—before replying. "My husband lives near Schenectady."

Rick Rofihe was born in Bridgewater, Nova Scotia, Canada in 1950 and has lived in New York City. His fiction has appeared in The New Yorker and his nonfiction in The New York Times. His first collection of stories, FATHER MUST, was published by Farrar, Straus and Giroux. A Whiting Award winner, he has taught fiction writing at Columbia University. He lives in Canada.